ALSO BY ANN RINALDI:

Amelia's War

Mine Eyes Have Seen

THE QUILT TRILOGY
A Stitch in Time
Broken Days
The Blue Door

The Second Bend in the River

In My Father's House

Wolf By the Ears

Girl in Blue

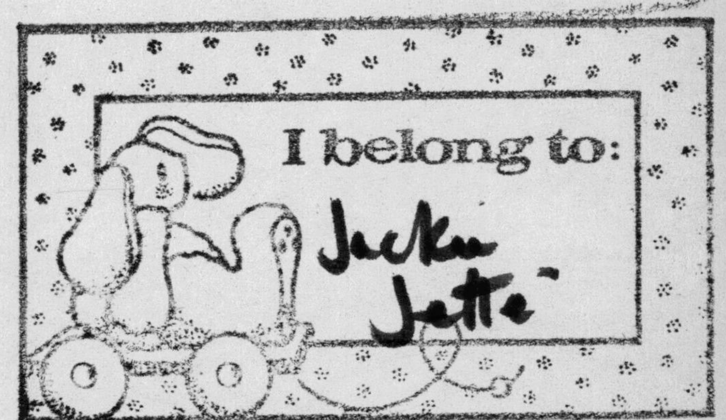

Girl in Blue

BY ANN RINALDI

SCHOLASTIC INC.
New York Toronto London Auckland Sydney
Mexico City New Delhi Hong Kong Buenos Aires

ISBN 0-439-67646-0

12 11 10 9 8 7 6 5 4 3 2 1 4 5 6 7 8 9/0

Printed in the U.S.A. 01

First trade paperback printing, May 2004

For the librarians at
Somerset County Library
in New Jersey,
for their help and patience
over the years.

CHAPTER ONE

May 8, 1861, Casey's Mill, Michigan

THE GIRL, SARAH LOUISA, SAT BY THE OPEN WINDOW IN the back bedroom that belonged to her brother. She sat in the rocker and rested the barrel of the Winchester .44 rifle on the sill. Its wood felt solid in her hands. Every so often she'd run her fingers over the fancy engraving of the girl on the stock, which was near worn now from so much use. How many times she'd sat in the woods, huddled in the brush, passing her hands over that girl, with a deer in her sights when hunting food for her family.

She called the gun Fanny, after the heroine in *Fanny Campbell, the Female Pirate Captain*, a book given to her by a peddler when she was thirteen. Fanny cut off her curls. She put on a short blue jacket. She went aboard ship as a man. And nevermore was she beholden to anyone.

Ever since the day she and her sister Betsy had been sent to the fields to plant potatoes in a patch of land far from the house and had taken the book with them, Sarah had been planning her escape. Never would she forget the way she felt when she read it. Like an angel had touched her with a live coal. And now, a little over two years later, it was still burning inside her.

At that moment, in the bundle at her feet, Sarah had a pair of scissors, taken from Ma's sewing basket. The time would soon be upon her when she would cut off her own curls.

In the potato field that day thirteen-year-old Sarah Louisa Wheelock had become Fanny. And in the more than two years that followed while she patiently hoed her father's fields, milked his cows, cleaned out his barn, helped slaughter his hogs, hunted game for his table, mended his fences, and took the cuffs and insults he gave her, she buried her anger. Especially when he made her kneel on the floor at the table while he ate, because her chores weren't done right. And she planned and plotted for this day.

This day when she would leave her father's place forever. And now it had come. Sooner than she had expected, but that, too, was her father's misdeed. Because now he had another job for her, a job she was not going to do. A job she would die before doing.

He planned for her to wed Ezekiel Kunkle, a farmer whose spread was south of theirs. All her life Sarah Louisa had known Ezekiel Kunkle. She'd known his worn-down wife, Nancy, who'd died of the milk-sick six months past. Sarah Louisa had been sent by her father to help care for the children at the time of the funeral. Even stayed over the night, against her mother's objections. "Isaac, that man has notions about our Sarah," Ma had said in one of the rare moments when she made bold to go against her husband. "I don't like the way he eyes her."

Her father had only chuckled.

"Don't worry, Ma," Sarah Louisa had said, knowing that her father was already plotting for her to wed Ezekiel, so there would be another hand on the farm. "I can take care of myself."

She had, too. Hit Ezekiel in the head with a fry pan the next morning when he tried to touch her while she was making breakfast for his three brats.

He was thirty-five if he was a day, tall, with a beard below his chin, a long jaw that all the time chewed, rotten teeth, and breath that smelled of whiskey. You needed to get a draught of clean cold air, just from standing downwind of him.

Twice already he'd come to call. And twice, "walking her out" he'd again tried to put his hands on her. When she'd told her father, he'd become angry and told her to stop making up lies. "He's a good man!" he'd yelled. "Helped me with the harvest last fall, didn't he? I'll hear no slander of him." Then he'd made her kneel on the floor by the hearth that night while everyone ate supper. For lying.

Now, Ezekiel was coming to call again, with her father's permission. Her ma and pa, and her sister Betsy, who helped Sarah with the chores but never did anything wrong in their father's eyes, had gone to Meeting. Below stairs her brother, Benjamin, was resting. He was having one of his spells, so he was excused from church.

Sarah knew she wasn't going to let Ezekiel Kunkle put his hands on her again today. And laugh while he did it. And say, "Your pa wants me in the family, so you'd best be good." She knew, too, that she couldn't depend on Ben for help. What could Ben do? She loved Benjamin, but it was part his fault that she was in this mess. Her father had wanted strapping sons, to till his soil. He got three daughters, and Benjamin, whose spine was sick, who did his best, but whose best was not enough.

Clarice, the oldest, was wed to Tobias Munday, had one baby, and lived over the wooded hill. It was up to Sarah Louisa and Betsy to do the chores. Betsy, fifteen, was as strong in the limbs as Sarah, but more given to courting boys and worrying about how she looked than to caring if the family lived or died.

"You ought to wed Ezekiel," she'd said more than once to Sarah. "He's not so bad, and with this war and all the young men going off, why you'll be an old maid before you get anyone else who wants you. And we could sure use his hands on this farm."

"Wed him yourself," Sarah had told her.

"I would, if Pa'd let me. I'd do anything to get out of these fields."

"You know what Ma always says, Betsy. There's a price to pay for everything."

"Sometimes it's worth paying," Betsy had returned. "And if Ma had learned that, she wouldn't be in the mess she's in."

"Don't talk against Ma," Sarah would order whenever the conversation took such a turn, as it often did. "I won't have it." Though she herself had wondered what would have been if Ma had been willing to pay the price of standing up to Pa.

When they worked in the fields and barn, the girls wore

men's clothing. Even when they drove the wagon to town, full of milk cans to be shipped down Lake Michigan to small towns below, they wore men's clothing. Ma said it would protect them around the docks. But many times on the way, Betsy would change into her woolen skirt and puff-sleeved Garibaldi blouse, and go around town while Sarah saw the milk cans handed on board and collected the money for them.

Sarah Louisa didn't mind the work. She took pride in her accomplishments, in being the best shot in the county, in knowing she could ride and swim better than the Bronson brothers in her town of Casey's Mill, between Flint and Pontiac.

She could build a fire in the rain. Live out in the wild on her wits if she had to.

But she would not kneel one more time by her father's side at the table while he shoved food in his mouth, with no more care than a hog, as her stomach rumbled with hunger.

She knew if she stayed around much longer she'd do or say something terrible. Then he'd take it out on her ma. There'd be shouting, throwing of things, even blows to her mother. Ma was so downtrodden she couldn't even name pride in her own accomplishments. Not even the way neighbors came to her for fixin' when they were taken ill. And for remedies.

The sun was ripe in the hard blue sky now over the newly-planted corn. It should be near noon. Ezekiel had told her father he'd come at noon, to court her. He'd told her that last Sunday at Meeting.

"I'll be a waiting with Fanny," she told Kunkle. "You dare come across the creek at the end of the south field and you'll feel Fanny's sting in your nether parts."

He'd laughed in her face. And looked her up and down like he was buying a horse. Said he liked a saucy woman. It added spice to a man's life. So sure of himself he was. So sure of her father's backing. It rankled her so, the way he thought he had a right to her.

It was two hundred yards to the creek, where she expected to sight him. She knew she could hit him from here. But she also knew she was not going to shoot him. Shooting deer or rabbits or pheasants for the family table was one thing. Shooting a man with three children because you didn't want to wed him was another.

She would scare him, though. That she knew she could do.

But she also knew then that she'd have to leave today. She had it all planned. She was going to Flint. Her ma had planned it, bless her, though her ma knew nothing about how she intended to scare off Ezekiel.

Ma had a sister in Flint who owned a millinery shop.

Ma had written to Aunt Annie and asked her to apprentice Sarah Louisa. It was all arranged.

So Ma thought. And this was the part that made Sarah Louisa a little guilty, the way she felt when she was about to shoot a doe and had to see the look in the animal's large molasseslike eyes. Sarah had no mind to work in a millinery shop. Fuss with hats all day? Help a lady decide what color ribbon to put on a bonnet? Not as long as she had breath in her body.

So she was going to Flint, but she had another plan. So bold that when she brought it to mind it was like diving in the cold creek on a hot summer day. But she'd done that enough and a half. And she could do this. She'd been studying on it ever since that day in early April when little Georgie Branwith came running across the creek waving a paper in his hand and yelling something about Fort Sumter.

Ever since a week later when the newspaper had it that Lincoln had called for seventy-five thousand men. And at supper Benjamin looked near tears. "I'd go if it weren't for this back," he'd said bitterly.

Ever since Clarice had paid a visit and said her husband was talking about enlisting in the Flint Union Greys.

Now she waited patiently, closed her eyes in the sun's warmth, and near dozed. Then she heard Mose, the family's best hunting dog, start to raise a ruckus and she knew it'd be Ezekiel, coming to claim her, and that if she let him come this day, she'd be lost.

She opened her eyes, accustomed them to the brightness outside, narrowed them to hone in on the figure on the horse just this side of the woods and t'other side of the creek beyond the field.

She raised the rifle and rested it on her shoulder. Its weight was familiar to her. She'd hold off until he crossed the creek. Only fair, she told herself. Make sure he was of a mind to come. Then she'd give him some spice. He'd know she meant what she said about not coming to call.

Had he sighted her at the upstairs window? Was he daring her to shoot? As she'd done so many times in the past hunting deer or possum, Sarah Louisa leaned forward, closed one eye, and took careful aim. He was coming toward the house now, bold as brass. In the quietness of the Sabbath fields she was sure she could hear his horse's snort.

She aimed at his floppy hat and saw it fly off his head. Saw him pull up on the horse's reins, stare at the house, shake a fist at her. Then she put down the gun and ran downstairs.

CHAPTER TWO

May 3, The Next Hour, Casey's Mill, Michigan

OF COURSE, THE BLAST OF THE WINCHESTER INSIDE the house was like the final judgment day Pa was always warning them about. Sarah's first thought was for Benjamin, sleeping in the parlor. She picked up her bundle of clothing, shoved the book about Fanny the pirate inside and ran downstairs. Outside Mose was taking on like old Chief Pontiac himself was attacking. Ben came, dazed, out of the parlor. Sarah could see the fever was upon him.

"What happened?"

"Nothing to worry about, Ben. I was polishing Pa's gun and it went off."

He gave her a queer look. Fever and all, he didn't believe her, not the way Sarah handled a gun.

"That's the right of it," she said.

He shrugged.

"You got the fever bad, Ben?"

"The chills is all."

She knew she didn't have much time. An hour at most to take her leave, and there were things to be done. But before she did anything, she made a strong cup of pennyroyal tea for her brother. Put a bit of butterfly-weed root in it. Sarah Louisa had learned such skills from her ma. In her bundle she even had a few remedies. When Ben was settled down with the tea, she ran outside. In one hand she had the Winchester and in the other a scrap of squirrel dumpling, left over from last night's supper.

As she passed Mose, she threw him the scrap of squirrel dumpling without stopping. That quieted him down right quick. Then she ran to the end of the field where Ezekiel was pacing, waiting for her. The first thing she noticed was that in one hand he had his skinning knife, which he had removed from its sheath.

"You female polecat! You near kilt me!"

"If I wanted to, I would have, Zeke. I told you not to come this morning, didn't I?"

"Your pa give permission! He'll take a horsewhip to you when I tell him this. Your pa wants us to wed. That's what this is about! It's why I come!" He shouted at her, waving his hand with the knife in it.

"My pa wants help with the farm, more than I can give!" she shouted back. "And you want help raising your passel of little ones. And this farm for your own. That's what this is all about, Zeke."

They circled each other, like two wolves, taking each other's measure. Sarah clutched the Winchester in her hands and kept her eyes on the skinning knife. You never could tell with Zeke. Many was the time over the last few years that she'd seen Nancy turn her face to hide a purple bruise. Sarah's heart was beating like a rabbit's being chased by Mose. "You'll never put your hands on me again, Zeke Kunkle."

"I was fixin' to wed you," he half whined. "Proper like. We wuz promised."

"I never promised you anything."

"Your pa did."

"Well, we don't have slavery here in Michigan, Zeke, in case you haven't heard about that."

Anger flooded his bewhiskered face. "I brung you these." He tossed a bouquet of wildflowers onto the ground between them.

It was the first Sarah had paid mind to them. "Flowers in one hand and a knife in the other? Doesn't that seem odd to you, Zeke?"

"Only oddment about all of this is that a woman should shoot at the man she's promised to. I oughta leave you a scar. Slash that pretty face of yours, is what I oughta do."

She saw the pupils of his eyes get smaller. "Put the knife away, Zeke," she said calmly. "Get on your horse and go home to your children."

He gripped it tighter, swung it back and forth a few times, then put it back in its sheath. "I'll be back," he said. "When your pa gits done with you, you'll come a'runnin' to me, you'll see."

Then, slowly, he mounted his horse. "I'll be back, Sary," he said. It was more a threat than a promise.

She stood only a moment in the field to watch as he slowly turned the horse and made his way back across the creek. She blinked at the flowers strewn among the newly-planted corn. Then she turned and ran back to the house.

Ben was on the porch, waiting for her. "What happened to him?" he asked.

"Sent him home." She brushed past him and went into the house. He followed.

"Pa's gonna be loaded for bear when he finds out you shot at him, Sarah."

"It'll be all right," she said. "I'm going to ride to Flint. Stay with Aunt Annie a few days. By the time I get back Pa'll be calmed down."

"Ma know you're goin'?"

"Ma arranged it, but let her do the telling."

Ben was uncommon tall. And skinny. Ma always said it was because he was so tall that his spine wasn't straight. "Can't hold all of him up," Ma said. Sarah Louisa had always thought what Ben's spine couldn't hold up was the woeful look on his face. And the bigness of his heart. Something hurt in her every time she looked at him. Every time she saw him dragging himself around to slop the hogs or sweep the porch, or sitting there on the porch stuffing corn shucks with sausage to be hung in the smokehouse, she thought her heart would break.

What would happen to Ben? Already he was seventeen. If it wasn't for the books he read, lent to him by Mr. Roane, the schoolteacher, likely he'd go daft.

One more reason why she was leaving. Too many things around this place had the poison about them and Sarah Louisa could do nothing about it. She made Ben another cup of tea, settled him on the sofa in the parlor, and gathered her things. Then she stood there with her bundle in one hand and Pa's gun in the other.

"Someday, Ben," she said, "I'll have a place of my own. A life of my own. And you can come live with me."

He smiled at her wanly. "You're skedaddelin', aren't you, Sarah?"

"Like I told you. I'll be back."

She met his sad brown eyes and saw her own lie in them. And her own truth. Then she turned and went out into the May sunshine, to the barn where her horse Max was already saddled. She'd have to leave him on the sly with Aunt Annie, with a note so he could get back to the farm. The Flint Union Greys weren't cavalry. And anyway, she loved Max too much to take him to war.

Before she rode out the gate she whirled Max around to take one final look at the house, sitting snug under the newly budding trees, smoke curling from its two chimneys. It was not home to her. It was a place to get away from. I misdoubt, she thought, that the slaves in the South been worst treated than me.

With that thought she rode off, careful to follow the trails through the woods she knew so well, so she wouldn't meet with Ma, Pa, and Betsy on their way home from Meeting.

CHAPTER THREE

May 5, 1861, Flint, Michigan

SARAH STOOD TO THE SIDE OF THE ROWDY CROWD assembled outside the recruiting office on the corner of Saginaw and Kearsley streets. It was Tuesday afternoon. Sarah had worked all morning in the shop, fashioning the red, white, and blue rosettes that bore the words THE UNION AND THE CONSTITUTION.

Aunt Annie and two helpers had, the whole previous week, embroidered those words in gold thread on the tails of the rosette ribbons. Sarah's fingers were pricked and sore from making the rosettes, which every woman in Flint intended to pin on the coat of a soldier on the morrow when they gathered at this very corner to march off.

Aunt Annie was still working in the shop with her helpers, making the last of the rosettes, but had sent Sarah out to run some errands. "You look like you have the need of some fresh air, child. Go, though I'm ashamed to let you out in that dress. Have you nothing fit to wear?"

"I tore it on the ride here," Sarah lied, though it pained her to lie to Aunt Annie, with her white hair, sparkling eyes, and broad bosom. She was a widow, but better off by far than Ma, Sarah saw right off. She lived above her shop, had a man friend in a swallow-tailed coat, wasn't above sharing a small beer with him, and never got her feathers ruffled, far as Sarah could see.

She'd told Sarah that she'd never felt so free as when she became a widow. Secretly, Sarah suspected that Aunt Annie would approve of her plan to run off with the Flint Union Greys, maybe even outfit her for it if she knew. But she couldn't entangle Aunt Annie that way. No, she'd leave a note and say she was going to see if she could become a nurse in Washington. She had it all planned.

"Well, I'm too stout to give you the loan of one of my dresses, so as soon as this rosette business is over I'll stitch you up a couple of new ones," Aunt Annie had promised.

Sarah had done the errands, the green grocer, the apothecary, the mercantile. All along the streets she'd seen the posters nailed up, screaming out the need for army recruits.

EIGHTEEN OR OVER! they fair shouted at you.

The recruiting office was in the armory, a log building at the corner of Saginaw and Kearsley. Because the day was pleasant, the sergeant had a table set up outside. The line of recruits extended all the way around the corner into the alley, where Sarah stood a bit away from them. She watched and listened as, one by one, the smooth-faced fearful youths took their place in front of the desk to answer the sergeant's rapid-fire questions.

Can you make music?

Where you from?

Can you shoot a gun?

Over eighteen?

Music seemed to be the magic word, Sarah noted. The army needed drummers, buglers. Some who answered yes to that question immediately got a pen shoved into their hands. They did not look eighteen to Sarah.

If only she could drum, she thought. Or bugle. But the skills she had were far superior. She knew how to tend wounds, shoot a gun, ride, swim, stand up to the sun of a long summer day. Weren't such talents needed?

She stood for half an hour watching, listening, as one after another the young men shuffled up to the desk and were either accepted or turned away. Especially, she watched the younger ones. Those turned away, she decided, did not look the recruiter square in the eye, did not stand tall and confident. Or shuffled their feet or looked abashed or ashamed. Or could scarce speak plain. Just couldn't stand up to that bearded, rough-voice recruiting sergeant when he asked, "Over eighteen?"

Others did. And some of them didn't look eighteen to Sarah. What made the difference? Why did some hold up in front of that bear of a man and others crumble?

It was the lie some could not tell, she decided. They worried it like a bone, like Sarah did. They wanted to join. Maybe, like her, they even needed to join. Like Sarah, they had been brought up churchgoing. To lie was wrong. Of course, she had learned to lie to protect herself at home. There were times you either lied to Pa or you would be picking yourself up off the floor. Sarah didn't know much about God from her regular churchgoing. But she was fairly sure God didn't approve of Pa to begin with.

But how did you lie to the U.S. government? For sure, this bear of a man represented the government, didn't he?

She didn't concern herself as much with the larger lie, passing as a man. She knew she could do that. Hadn't she spent years now doing a man's work? Dressing in a man's clothes? Likely she could shoot and ride better than all these recruits. Anyway, there were no laws yet about passing as a man. But there were laws about lying about your age to an army recruiter.

So, she calculated standing there, if I can get past the age business, I will be all right.

Then, as sure as if God had heard her thoughts, the way came to her. A voice behind her, soft. "Miss?"

She turned. He was young, his face smooth, he looked younger than Ben even. "Yes?"

"Excuse me, Miss, but I was wonderin'. Could you hold my haversack for a minute? The street is kind of muddy."

Where they stood was more in an alley beside the armory, but she didn't mark the distinction. She took the haversack, then watched in fascination as he unlaced one of his boots and slipped a piece of paper inside. Before he put his stockinged foot back in she saw that there was a number on the paper.

Eighteen.

The foot went in, the boot was laced. He stood and grinned at her. "Thank ye, Miss. I'm beholden."

"What does it mean?" she asked.

"Beg pardon?"

"The number in your shoe. What does it mean?"

"Why, Miss, it's a trick that works. I want to enlist, you see. But I'm just sixteen. It's wrong to lie, so I've been taught. I just couldn't wash away the guilt if I did. So I put that paper in my boot. Then, when the sergeant there asks me if I'm over eighteen, the way he does, why I say yes. And I'm not lying."

"You're not?"

"Course not, Miss. I'm *over* eighteen. Don't you see?" The grin widened, showing perfect white teeth.

"Yes," Sarah Louisa breathed softly. "Yes, I see. Good luck to you."

"Thank ye, Miss. I've got to run. The Flint Union Greys are attached to the 2nd Michigan. And they leave for Detroit day after tomorrow."

He bowed and ran to take his place in line. Sarah stood waiting, though it was growing late and she was long since expected back at Aunt Annie's. When the young man's turn came to stand before the desk she held her breath. But she needn't have worried. The sergeant fired the questions at him. He stood tall and straight and answered.

"Over eighteen?" the sergeant barked.

"Yes, Sir."

The sergeant shoved a pen at him. "Sign here. Two-year enlistment."

Sarah Louisa turned and started for her Aunt Annie's

house. She knew she'd have to do it soon. She and Ma had agreed that Ma would tell Pa she was staying at Aunt Annie's for a few days because Aunt Annie was feeling poorly. Then Aunt Annie would write Pa, saying she couldn't do without the services of her niece, and she'd pay her well and send the money to him. That part rankled Sarah, that her pa would get money she worked so hard for. But it was necessary to keep him at bay until she learned the trade. Then, Aunt Annie and Ma had agreed, Aunt Annie would send her on down to Washington City, where she could work for a friend of Aunt Annie's in another millinery shop.

Sarah was afraid that as God made the corn nubbins grow, Pa would be after her if she didn't return in two or three days.

"Let him try," Aunt Annie had said.

Sarah trusted her. But she knew she'd have to do it soon because the 2nd Michigan was leaving day after tomorrow.

May 5, The Evening, Aunt Annie's shop, Flint, Michigan

Sarah had learned some matters of value in the afternoon she spent watching the men signing on. She had searched for her brother-in-law, Clarice's husband Tobias

Munday. But he was nowhere to be seen. Of course, she realized he could have already signed on and now be with the numbers of men either in the armory or camping in the field at the end of town. She knew her chances of being discovered were twofold if Tobias was in the Flint Union Greys. But then, the regiment was so big and Tobias stood out so, with broad shoulders, great height, and red hair. She would be able to spot him if he came near.

Clarice had not wanted Tobias to volunteer. And he would do anything for Clarice. Sarah knew that. It was one of the reasons why Clarice, so long ordered about by their father, had married him. Tobias had rescued her, nothing less. Sarah was counting on the fact that he would not leave for war. Not just yet.

The other thing she had learned was that she would need some sort of disguise. She was good at disguises, as well as mimicry. The few times she'd been able to make Ma laugh was when she'd imitated Ezekiel Kunkle, even deepening her voice and spitting on the ground. And she had played Topsy in her school's presentation of *Uncle Tom's Cabin.*

So now, while townfolk strolled the boardwalk outside the front windows in Aunt Annie's shop in the sweet May darkness, Sarah Louisa worked feverishly behind closed shutters by the light of a single kerosene lamp. All around her were the innards of Aunt Annie's business, ribbons, lace, jars of paste she had concocted, straw hats, swatches of velvet and silk. There had been a run on red, white, and blue ribbons today. Every other woman in Flint, it seemed, had wanted her hat trimmed for tomorrow.

But Sarah was working with black hair. It was a plan she'd conceived working in the shop that day. Some women came to Aunt Annie for extra curls to cascade from under their bonnets. So Aunt Annie bought hair and fashioned it into wigs.

After supper Aunt Annie's swallow-tailed gentleman friend had come by to take her with him. He was the bandmaster in Flint and tomorrow the band would play while the soldiers assembled for ceremonies before leaving.

"If I don't come home this night, don't worry," Aunt Annie had told her. "I and some other women will be keeping them in food while they practice."

How Sarah envied her aunt's freedom to come and go as she pleased, beholden to no man. Imagine Ma saying such.

She took the opportunity to go downstairs to the shop. Now she was fashioning a narrow goatee and mustache. She had already cut off her curls and, every so often while she worked, she shook her head, unaccustomed to the absence of the dark mass that had always feathered her neck. She had fed and said good-bye to Max, who was now munching his supper in the small barn behind the house and shop.

She had already written the note for Aunt Annie. It was in her pocket.

All that was left was to sign up. She decided she had best do it now. She had heard that the recruiting sergeant would be behind his desk until ten o'clock this evening. In a corner of the shop, behind the counter that held the last of the rosettes, she pulled off the torn calico dress and stood tucking her shirt into her trousers. In her boot she'd already put the small scrap of paper that said eighteen. She knew it was foolish. But she needed all the luck she could get.

Carefully, in front of a small mirror, she pasted the small goatee and mustache on her face with spirit gum. That mole on her left cheekbone was a problem, she minded. People could always identify you by a mole. Maybe in the army she'd meet a doctor who could take it off.

No, best stay away from doctors. They saw things other people didn't.

She studied herself in the mirror. Then it came to her. Soldiers didn't get a chance to shave every day and with the rest of her face baby-smooth, how could she explain a goatee? She decided against the mustache, too. She'd take them along, though. See how things went.

She took the note for Aunt Annie out of her pocket and left it on the counter. Then she picked up her bundle, went out the front door, locked it, and headed for the corner of Saginaw and Kearsley.

CHAPTER FOUR

May 5, Evening, Recruiting Office, Flint, Michigan

"I, NEDDY COMPTON, DO SOLEMNLY SWEAR, IN THE presence of Almighty God, that I will support the Constitution of the United States, and maintain it and my country's flag, if necessary, with my life; that I will obey the commands of my superior officers while in service, and will defend and protect my comrades in battle to the best of my physical ability."

✦ ✦ ✦

The recruiting sergeant had scarce looked at Sarah. She'd stood, knees shaking, hands sweating as she clutched the Winchester.

It had been worse than facing Pa when the cows' stalls were not cleaned out right.

"Name?"

"Neddy Compton."

"Where you from?"

"Little town between Pontiac and Flint. My family owns a farm."

"You over eighteen?"

Sarah had met a young man by the name of Sam only within the last hour who'd told her another tactic. Said it worked every time. "Don't rightly know, sir. My ma, she died when I was seven. There were so many of us Pa lost count. Said I was eighteen."

There wasn't a recruiting sergeant in a hundred miles, Sam had said, who could let somebody like that get away. They needed men, bad. Who could fault him?

"Can you shoot anything with that thing?"

"Kept my family in food the last three years," Sarah said.

"Do you drink? Got a cough or anything?"

"No, sir."

"Ever spit up blood?"

"No, sir."

The sergeant shoved the pen and paper at Sarah. She did what she could to keep her hand from shaking as she signed.

There was a doctor. But only certain ones got examined. Sam had told her that, too. The ones who coughed, who looked sickly. The others were passed right on down the line.

The pine knot torches glowed against the spring night, which flowed around Sarah like a sweet pillow as she held up her right hand and took the oath.

She was now Neddy Compton.

She stood between two lanky youths, holding her Winchester while she took the oath. There were at least two dozen just sworn in, but only three or four had rifles. There were no uniforms, would be none until they arrived in Washington, they'd been told. There were forage caps distributed, but they were baggy and made of cheap fabric. They were dark blue and had a visor. The cap was enough for Sarah. It hid her short curls.

Colonel W. M. Fenton, who'd organized the Greys, now stood before them. He had a uniform, shiny and blue, complete with sword and gold buttons and gold fringe on his shoulders.

"Gentlemen, this is a solemn and impressive occasion. We expect you not only to adhere to your sacred oath, but to comport yourselves so you will be a pride to your regiment. I especially exhort you to strict cleanliness and temperance in both meals and drink."

Sarah was hungry already. Supper at Aunt Annie's seemed hours past. She had heard that rations on the march were salt pork, hardtack, and coffee. She had heard that the 2nd Michigan would be completed when they arrived in Fort Wayne, Detroit, that they would leave for Washington on the sixth of June.

"You are the first volunteer infantry regiment to be formed in Michigan," Colonel Fenton was telling them. "Tomorrow, the 2nd Michigan Infantry will be completed with the arrival of companies from Hudson, Battle Creek, Adrian, Niles, Constantine, East Saginaw, and Kalamazoo. Tomorrow we form up in this very spot to march!"

They were dismissed to go back to their homes or bed down in the armory. Sarah knew she could not go back to Aunt Annie's. She was counting on the fact that Aunt Annie would not be home this night, and by tomorrow, when they formed up with the other regiments, she would be lost in the crowd.

Tomorrow they would be given blue Union caps, the

colonel had said. Right now she had to go inside the armory, where there was hot coffee and sergeants were distributing blankets, canteens, and equipment for cooking and eating.

She took her place in line inside for her equipment. Men were just throwing their blankets down on the floor in the armory. Sarah staked out a corner and went to have coffee and cake being served by some town women. Then she joined two of the youngest-looking fellows as they stood around sipping their coffee and munching their cake.

"Heard we'll be reviewed by President Lincoln hisself when we get to Washington City," the one called Frank said.

"I heard to watch out for them New York regiments," his companion answered. "Seems they're Bowery boys. The one requirement they got for enlistment is that you do time in prison." He grinned at Sarah to include her in the conversation, then stuck out his hand. "Daniel Hooks," he said.

Sarah was sure to look him straight in the eye. She had determined she would not cower, shuffle, mumble, or do anything to cause suspicion to be cast upon her. "Neddy Compton," she said.

"Where'd you get the rifle?" Frank asked.

"My pa's. He let me take it," Sarah answered.

"Heard we'll be issued Springfields," Daniel Hooks said, "but fer sure, that's a beauty."

Sarah sipped her coffee. It was hot and sweet. She needed it. She felt as if she'd just run a hundred-mile footrace and won. They accepted her! There was no question! She was filled with a sense of elation.

She just stood there sipping her coffee for a while and listening to snatches of conversation from the small groups all around her. She heard words like, "truth and freedom," and "putting down the rebellion," and "going after those damned Rebels."

All these young men believed in the cause, she decided. From the sound of it, some were taken with the very romance of preserving the Union. She let her gaze roam the room. The flickering light shaded some faces, emboldened others. There was an undercurrent of talk, low and almost respectful. She felt a kinship already with these two dozen souls who had come from farms and shops and schools to defend what they believed in. She would do well here, she decided. She had done the right thing.

Still, she slept fitfully that night. The floor was hard under her blanket. At one end of the room was a hearth and a glowing fire. When she did sleep, she dreamed of home. Her mother's face, Betsy's, even Ezekiel's, though that part of the dream had no good feelings. When she woke in the night she could not mind, at first, where she was. Around her men snored. One was writing by the glow of a single candle. Some were whispering. The room smelled of men, their sweat, the outdoors that clung to their clothing, the horse smell that attached itself to some, and tobacco, even whiskey. Someone at the other end of the room had a flask and she saw two men drinking. Against the rules, she knew, but she also knew she must cast a blind eye to such things.

Some girls would have been fearful in such surroundings. Others, bedazzled. Sarah was neither. At this particular moment in her life men had no appeal for her. The only ones she'd known besides hair-pulling schoolboys had been her father and her brother. Her father she hated, and he represented all men to her. Her brother she loved the way she loved Betsy. She was fond of saying she would never wed, would never become a lovesick calf, running after some man, as she'd seen her sister Betsy do.

She wanted to be independent, earn her own way, be free of all bonds.

Sarah turned over on the hard floor and went back to sleep.

May 6, Midmorning, Outside the Recruiting Office, Flint, Michigan

The sunlight was so bright that even the visor of the new blue Union cap did not shield her eyes from it. The colonel barked orders and already the new recruits knew enough to "shoulder arms." Those without guns had been issued them. Springfields. Everyone had been issued bayonets. Across the street was a crowd of women and children and older men. Almost every woman wore a red, white, and blue ribbon on her bonnet. The children held flags.

Sarah saw Aunt Annie's swallow-tailed gentleman friend on a podium, baton in hand, leading his band in "The Star-Spangled Banner."

The notes drifted hauntingly on the morning air. Then, when it was over and everyone cheered, the Methodist pastor, Reverend Mr. Joslin, was introduced. One by one, the Flint Union Greys were given a copy of the New Testament. Then some ladies from town came by with the rosettes and pinned them on the coats of the soldiers.

Sarah's knees were so weak she thought she'd faint, expecting to see Aunt Annie do the pinning. But Aunt Annie was standing near the bandstand, looking admiringly up at her swallow-tailed gentleman. Sarah stood at attention as the rosette, maybe one she had even made herself, was pinned on her.

Then there was a presentation of revolvers to the officers. And the ceremony was over.

They were ready to march.

More music. As Sarah filed by, surrounded by her newfound companions, she passed Aunt Annie, who was watching from the wooded walk.

"Eyes ahead!" Lieutenant William Turver ordered.

Sarah didn't have to be told twice. She couldn't bear to look at Aunt Annie. Anyway, she couldn't have seen her for the tears.

CHAPTER FIVE

May 25, Fort Wayne, Detroit, Michigan

MARCH! MARCH! MARCH, OLD SOLDIER, MARCH! *Hayfoot, strawfoot, belly full of bean soup, March, old soldier, march!*

Sarah knew that if she ever heard the words again, she'd throw up. Every day, for the last three weeks, they'd been out on the drill field, in the early summer heat, toting around their rifles, *not firing them,* the way she'd have the troops doing all along, if she were in charge, until this last week.

Half the troops couldn't hit the targets. The other half

were so untaught they didn't know their left foot from their right. Kept tripping and turning the wrong way and bumping into one another for the first two weeks of training. Some didn't know how to clean their rifles. Sarah herself had taught two young men who were so afraid to handle the Springfields she was sure the first time they did they would shoot themselves in the head.

Strawfoot was the name for a new recruit. Sarah didn't blame the sergeants for any name they put on some of the men. Her two tentmates, for instance, deserved the most demeaning name she could think of.

The first week they'd taken every instance to lie around and smoke and revel in their uncombed hair, unbuttoned shirts, and unwashed tin plates. Apparently this was the first time they'd been on their own, away from their mamas, and they couldn't believe their good fortune.

"Beats clerkin' any day," the one had said.

"Beats farmin', too," from the other.

Their names were Jake Curran and Anthony Hill. They teased Sarah because she took her duties so seriously. Both were from Lansing. There was only one thing Sarah envied about them: They wrote home. She'd lie on her pallet at night and hear the scratching of their pens by candlelight as they wrote their adventures to their families.

"'Dear Ma,'" Jake read aloud one night from his own

letter, "'There's a group here from northern Pennsylvania. The 13th Pennsylvania reserves. They call themselves the Bucktails, because they decorated' — hey, Neddy, what's the spell of it?"

"Of what?" Sarah would ask from her end of the tent.

"Decorated."

So she'd spell the word. She did this all the time for both of them. And Jake would scratch the word down and continue reading: "'. . . they decorated their caps with strips of fur they got from a deer carcass in front of a butcher shop near their camp at Harrisburg.' Hey, Neddy, do Harrisburg have one *r* or two?"

From somewhere between the rows of tents would float the smell of fresh coffee. And the sound of a harmonica playing "Home Sweet Home." Sarah would get up then, so washed of feeling she'd think she'd just had a bath with her mama's lye soap. She could even smell lye soap as she made her way out of the tent and to the campfire where the coffee was bubbling.

She'd stay up late, talking with anybody who wanted to talk. One thing she had discovered by now was that it was easier to talk to the other men around a campfire at night than in the harsh light of day. You couldn't see the look in the other person's eyes, for one. And they couldn't see the look in yours. She'd go back to her tent late, after Jake and Anthony were asleep. She was tired, yes, exhausted from marching all day. But more tired from spelling words that she should have been writing to someone at home. If she stayed in the tent she'd only end up composing her own letter in her mind. Finishing it in her dreams. But it was all right being tired. Tomorrow they were leaving for Washington City.

May 26, Someplace in Ohio

It was raining. Water dripped from the shed of the train station, pinged onto barrels on nearby wagons, and soaked into their clothing. They had been given uniforms. Sarah now wore a long flannel shirt of blue, with the tails outside the gray pants. And new shoes.

What bothered the recruits was that they did not even know where they were. The train had stopped for food and the sign on the depot had been torn down. But a band awaited them, and so they were ushered off to line up in formation. It was someplace in Ohio, one of the recruits said. He recognized the countryside. Some ladies were coming toward them now, pulling small wagons carrying gigantic urns of coffee. Others had cake. Sarah hoped they didn't have to board before she got her treat.

There were rumors that the owners of the railroad were charging two cents a mile per soldier to transport them to Washington City. There were rumors that they'd run into trouble passing through Baltimore since Southern sympathy ran so high there.

Sarah no longer listened to rumors. She accepted her hot coffee and cornbread from a woman who looked a little bit like Aunt Annie and tried not to spill any of the hot liquid on herself as they marched off to board. She'd hoard the cornbread. There was rumor they might not get anything to eat all the way to Washington.

May 31, Baltimore

As the train rumbled through the countryside, past farms and railroad yards and the backs of city houses, all Sarah could think of, stuck in her seat against the grimy window, was, I've never been on a train before. I'm the first one in my family ever to do so. I wish I could write Ma. Or Benjamin. Benjamin would love to hear this. So many towns, so many houses, so many people, so many soldiers. My, Maryland is pretty. Pa should see these farms. He'd be less sour of tongue. Or maybe more so, since they seem so much more prosperous than ours.

Then came the outskirts of a town. Or a city. Through the window Sarah could see crowds in the streets. Then lining the tracks. As the train started to slow down, the blur of faces separated into people. People throwing things.

As a rock hit her window and careened off it, Sarah jumped and fell into the sleeping soldier next to her, a Pennsylvania boy, a Bucktail. His hat with the bit of deer fur on it fell onto his lap. "Watch yourself," he growled.

"I'm sorry," Sarah said, "but the rock scared me."

"Sounded like a shotgun. What are they doing?"

"Attacking us," Sarah said, "from what I can see."

They came to a slow, screeching, steam-enveloping halt. The crowd was on the platform now, shouting, fists raised, hurling stones, brickbats. A regiment of soldiers with drawn bayonets held them off the cars. The train halted less than ten minutes, then was on its way again. Afterward, Sarah heard that some rocks had come through the windows, hitting soldiers.

"Why?" she asked the sergeant who came through to reassure them.

"They're secessionists. About a month ago they attacked the 6th Massachusetts when they came through. Now it seems everyone is fair game."

As he spoke, a woman pushed her face next to the window and glared in at Sarah, her mouth forming obscene words. Her eyes bulged. Her fist shook. For the first time since she had left home Sarah felt a kernel of fear sprouting inside her. These people were civilians. What would the secessionists in uniform be like when they had guns in their hands?

The Bucktail next to Sarah went back to sleep. The train started again, picked up pace, and once more there was the beautiful Maryland countryside at dusk. Sarah saw a farmer herding his cows into the barn for the evening milking. She saw candlelight behind the farmhouse windows and felt such a depth of loneliness that she thought she would die.

May 31, Washington City

If Sarah thought she was no longer a green recruit after passing through the angry mob in Baltimore, when she saw Washington she felt as if she had "strawfoot" stamped on her forehead.

At first she felt the general excitement that ran through her car like a stream of warm water. Washington! President Lincoln! The White House! As if some signal had been given, the soldiers started to stand in the aisles as the train rocked into the depot. Necks craned and Sarah heard snatches of conversation.

"My older sister is here. Says she's gonna be a nurse. Did you ever hear such a notion? A woman nurse?"

"I was hoping to buy some flour to dress up our provisions. But they say it's up to twelve dollars a barrel here."

"My sister wrote home that if a person writes a letter to someone down south they risk investigation."

"Folderol! I heard the place is swarming with spies."

The regiments formed up once off the cars and marched through Washington Depot. It was huge and echoing, filled with soldiers arriving from the north and west. Sarah was surprised how heavy her haversack felt. Where were they going? How far? Word ran down the line. To someplace called Gales Woods, to stack their arms, to camp. Supper would be waiting.

Supper. Home. At this time at home she'd be going out to the barn to lock the doors for the night. The moon would be rising over the mountains. Her ma would be putting her bread dough to set for the morning. She could almost smell Ma's fresh bread. To keep the loneliness at bay, Sarah composed a letter in her mind.

"Dear Ma, Well, we're here in Washington City. It's dark, though the streets are lit with gaslight. As we march through the muddy streets, I can see soldiers everywhere. Hundreds of them. Also the sidewalks are crowded with people, all kinds. Darkies, clerks, important-looking people and just plain onlookers, ragged newsboys hawking the Evening Star. *There*

are pigs in the street. Even geese. As we marched I passed some shanties and some homes that look like real palaces. The 1st Rhode Island marches right ahead of us. Behind us is the 13th Brooklyn. They are a common lot, bold and irreverent. I can see the half-finished Capitol in the distance. Bands seem to be playing all around and their sound is brittle in the air. Not comforting. Somebody said there are over 50,000 volunteers here. Ma, I can't believe I'm here. Ma, oh, how I wish I could send this letter to you."

May 31, Near midnight, Washington

There were Sibley tents on the hill, set up and waiting for them. It was starting to drizzle. For as far as Sarah could see there were tents and campfires and the dark forms of men, the smell of horses, the mute sounds of an occasional harmonica or, of a sudden, a loud laugh.

And then there were the people, civilians, who'd come to put the wash-kettles on the fires. Some held soup, some coffee. There were wagon-loads of bread cut into chunks, cheese, milk, even plum pudding.

"Welcome to Camp Winfield Scott," someone said. Sarah was directed to her tent. Her tentmate, whoever he was, had his gear already set in place. She set hers down and went to get some supper.

Soldiers, weary from the day's travel, weary from the

march, were dropping down anywhere, taking food from the matrons who brought it, being scolded by their superiors. "Find your tent, son." Some slept right where they fell and had to be shaken to be awakened.

June 1, Morning, Washington

When the bugler woke her at five it was still dark. But Sarah noted that the rain had stopped.

"You were asleep when I came in last night," a voice from across the tent said. "Name's Jimmy Cowles."

Sarah reached across the space between them and took the proffered hand.

"My company got in before yours," Cowles said. "You been assigned yet?"

"Assigned?" Sarah asked.

"I'm to be an orderly in charge of supplies for the hospital. First things first, though. The latrine's down by the ridge line, near the trees. Get there early enough and it won't stink so much. The food's not bad. And we'll have to fall in for dress parade after breakfast. I hear President Lincoln himself is coming to tour our camp today. Better get started. The tents get inspected. Want to walk down with me to the latrine?"

"No," Sarah said. "I think I'll straighten my part of the tent, first."

June 1, Midmorning, Washington

Sarah felt so stiff she thought she would break like a twig if anybody so much as bumped into her. The day had turned cloudless and blue. For miles in the distance, as she and hundreds around her stood at attention, all she could see were white tents, like cherry blossoms on the hills. She felt, with each breath she took, that she was breathing in unison with the men all around her. Flags snapped in the brisk breeze. Every so often, a horse bearing an officer would snort and bob its head and Sarah would hear the rattle of its bridle, but little else. From a distance over the hill came the sound of martial music.

She'd had breakfast, set her side of the tent to rights, put her uniform in order, and managed to visit the bushes a little away from the latrine. Two soldiers from the 13th Brooklyn saw her coming out of them and laughed.

"Shy, soldier? You'll get over it!" they called back at her as they went up the hill.

Now the President was coming.

Orders were barked all up and down the line. There was the uniform snap to attention, the shouldered muskets, bayonets gleaming in the sun.

Sarah was in the third row, but she caught full view of President Lincoln and his wife as they walked by. He was so tall, just as she'd heard tell of him. And his wife's hoop-skirt was so wide. He held her arm and they stopped on occasion to speak to a commander or a soldier in the line. The band was playing and then he turned to face Sarah's regiment and she saw the long nose, the sad eyes, heard the voice as he asked one soldier up front where he was from.

In her head Sarah was composing another letter home that she knew she would never write:

"Dear Ma, Today I came within five feet of Mr. Lincoln, President of these United States. He spoke to us. What surprised me most was that his voice didn't bark, the way our commanders do. He has a light voice and a face that looks like the ground after we plow it in spring. But it's in his eyes, Ma. You should see those eyes. He looks like he knows all the bad things that will happen."

She felt tears come to her eyes, and pride swell in her heart and rise with the jaunty music in the air. For the first time in her life she felt part of something outside herself, something larger than she could ever hope to be, something that might even go on if she fell in battle.

That afternoon there was a dress parade and they passed in view of the President.

Afterward she was given her assigned duties for the next month, until they went into battle.

Private Neddy Compton was to work with Private Jimmy Cowles, her tentmate, in one of the hospitals. He was to keep track of men from the 2nd Michigan who were sent there on sick call and write daily reports of their progress.

CHAPTER SIX

June 5, A Hospital in Washington

THE HOSPITAL SARAH WAS SENT TO WAS NO MORE THAN an extra-large tent set up under some trees on open land near the city. There were several of these tents within eye distance. And so it was that on a hot day, under a sky hung with low clouds, privates Neddy Compton and Jimmy Cowles reported to the assistant surgeon of hospital tent number five.

The first trouble had come to the Army of the Potomac even before the first battle. Typhoid fever. Already five men from the 2nd Michigan were stricken. Sarah's job, she'd been told, was to "see to them. Make sure they aren't slackers, but really sick. And as soon as they can stand on their feet have them report back to duty."

She was to find the assistant surgeon and give him this note, Colonel Fenton had told her. He handed her the note. "Give it to no one else but him," Fenton ordered.

Sarah found the assistant surgeon. He was the only one, besides two male nurses, in the tent hospital at midmorning when they got there. His name was Doctor William Hammond. He was a tall man with a long, thin nose, a high forehead, a full beard, and a scant amount of hair on the back of his head. And he looked, to Sarah, skittish, as if he were being pursued.

He read the note and glanced down at her. Or rather at Private Neddy Compton. "Slackers, hell," he said. "Apparently your commander knows nothing about typhoid." He gestured to the men lying on cots, at least twenty-five in the tent. "And if he did, he'd make sure the men used the latrines instead of relieving themselves all over the ground. And that they don't drink water from the nearby stream. All the camps are contaminated! With this heat, that's what causes typhoid and there's no slackers here!"

He was angry. Sarah felt herself blush then say, "Yes, Sir."

"You can see to the men of the 2nd Michigan in fifteen minutes. What are your orders for the rest of the day?"

"I have none, Sir."

"Well, you do now. Every time it rains, the water floods the floors in here. The drains outside the tent need to be dug deeper. You look like a strong lad. From a farm?"

"Yes, Sir. Michigan."

"Good, then you know about chickens."

"Chickens, Sir?"

"Yes." Then he gave a sharp whistle and out of nowhere appeared a small black boy with a bucket of water and a ladle. "One of the many who've already come to us across Rebel lines," he explained. Then, to the boy. "Nubbin, I want you to go with Private Compton this afternoon to the places I usually send you for food. You understand? You're to show Private Compton the right houses."

"Yassah." The boy was no more than eight years old, ragged and bright-eyed.

"They expect us to give men who have been struck by the sun or with high fevers pork, hard bread, and coffee," he said to Sarah. "I need chickens, bottles of blackberry wine, lemon syrup, jellies, brandy, groceries, even ice. You'll pack the ice in that straw over yonder. Nubbin knows where to beg for such supplies."

"Beg, Sir?" Sarah asked.

"Yes, Private. We beg. The ladies of Washington are most generous, if you present them with a proper face and tell them of my need. The ones Nubbin will take you to know me and have been generous to a fault. One is a doctor's wife. His name is Doctor Cornelius Boyle. If she isn't home, she'll be at his nearby drugstore. She should be good for a dozen bottles of blackberry wine and at least six of lemon syrup. The clergyman's wife should be good for the chickens. And so forth." He handed Sarah a list of names and addresses. "Just a moment."

He walked to the middle of the tent where a board table stood. On it sat a number of books and medicines. Sarah noted the clean wooden plank flooring, the clean ticking on the cots, the folded supply of sheets and blankets. When he came back he handed her a floppy straw farmer's hat and a clean handkerchief.

"Wear the hat out in the streets," he said.

"It isn't regulation, Sir."

In one stroke he took the blue Union cap from Sarah's head and replaced it with the floppy straw one. "It is now. I don't need another case of sunstroke. And when you visit the men from the 2nd Michigan, don't get too close. And mask your face with this." He handed her the handkerchief. She noted the initial *H* in the corner. It must be his own, she decided.

"Have yourself some lemonade and biscuits. You should be back here by four o'clock. No less. Don't make any stops except those that Nubbin tells you."

"Yes, Sir."

"And give that mule some water before you leave." He gestured to the mule pulling her wagon.

Sarah did as he said, thinking that if all Union doctors were like this man the Union was in good hands. With Nubbin beside her on the wagon seat they started off for the streets of Washington.

They drove past numerous hillsides with white tents, past the Washington Canal and the unfinished Washington Monument, where the army's horses and cattle grazed, and on to Pennsylvania Avenue and Center Market, where you could smell the fish being sold in the rear. There were soldiers everywhere, camping, walking, guarding, drilling. They passed dozens of Negroes building fortifications and, in the distance, supply trains moving slowly.

"My pappy works there," Nubbin said, pointing at the fortifications. He told Sarah they'd been in Washington since the firing on Sumter. "We got through the lines when the cannon wuz firin'," he said.

The streets were sultry, dusty, and smelly. Overhead the sky brooded, threatening rain. When they came on quality houses, the houses were shuttered against the heat. In front of the unfinished Capitol, Sarah could see muddy, almost swampy stretches of land. They passed groggeries from which came hurdy-gurdy music in the middle of the day, shanties where whole families dwelled. The city was an unfinished nightmare, she decided, and home to every drifter, outlander, mischief-maker, and would-be it could hold.

"This be C Street," Nubbin told her. "From here on to Washington Circle there be some quality houses. This be where our people at."

Sarah checked her list. True to Nubbin's word the addresses were handsome brick houses on C Street and Washington Circle. Here there were trees, wooden sidewalks, wrought-iron fences, and flowers.

"Stop here," Nubbin said in front of a pink-brick house with cream-colored shutters and window boxes. Sarah drew the mule to a halt.

"This be Dr. Boyle's," Nubbin told her. "You go to the front door, an' beg properlike."

Sarah got out of the wagon, brushed off her uniform trousers, took the straw hat off her head and put on the proper blue Union cap, then went up the steps to use the huge brass knocker. She had never begged for anything in her life, but when the door opened and the white-aproned maid stood there, frozen of face and grim of lip, Sarah took off her cap and made a little bow. "Ma'am, I come in the name of Doctor William Hammond. He remembers your mistress's past kindness and said we are in desperate need of some blackberry wine and lemon syrup for the men in his hospital."

The woman scowled at Sarah. "Where's the little colored boy who always comes?"

"There in the wagon, Ma'am. My name's Private Neddy Compton of the 2nd Michigan."

"Wait here." The woman disappeared into the cool, dark recesses of the house. Sarah heard a piano tinkling and smelled coffee and fresh baked bread from somewhere within. She caught a glimpse of carpets, a curved banister, and felt the ache of missing a home. Beds, she thought, clean sheets, a tub of hot water to bathe in, a kitchen stove. The loss cut inside her like a knife.

Within minutes the woman reappeared with a crate that held six bottles of blackberry wine, two of lemon syrup, and a brown jug. "Some lemonade for you both," she said. Then she handed Sarah a worn cup. "Can't have our fine soldiers drinking out of the same jug as the colored," she said.

Sarah had given no thought to where she'd be drinking from, she was so grateful for the lemonade. "I'm beholden, Ma'am. So is Doctor Hammond."

"Don't Ma'am me," the woman said. "I'm Sari the maid." And closed the door in Sarah's face.

They spent the afternoon making their way slowly from house to house. "Ice last," Nubbin told her, "so's it don't melt." And when they picked up the ice from the last house and she saw how carefully he wrapped it in straw and put an old parasol over it that the lady had given him, she thought he had more brains than any soldier she'd met yet in the Army of the Potomac. With the exception of Doctor Hammond.

As they were returning to the hospital an elegant carriage stopped on the other side of Pennsylvania Avenue and the driver beckoned to Sarah. "You there, Private!"

Sarah halted the mule.

"My mistress would speak to you."

At that moment the shade went up in the carriage and a woman of mid-age with a perky silk bonnet poked her head out the window. "Private, are you collecting food for the hospitals?"

"Yes, Ma'am," Sarah answered.

"I've seen your companion, the little colored boy, before. Come here, I have something for you."

Sarah hesitated, remembering Doctor Hammond's, "Don't make any stops except those that Nubbin tells you." She glanced at Nubbin, sitting behind her. In the bed of the wagon five chickens clucked nervously in a wire cage. Nubbin shrugged. "That's Mrs. Greenhow," he said.

"Who is she?"

"Lives on Sixteenth Street. Knows everybody 'portant in this town. Has lotsa parties. My ma sometimes helps out when she does."

"Well, it must be all right, then." Sarah hopped down from the wagon and quickly ran to the elegant carriage. The door opened and the woman Nubbin had called Mrs. Greenhow held out a bottle of sparkling wine. "My regards to Doctor Hammond," she said.

"You know him, Ma'am?" Sarah asked.

"I know of him. There isn't much that goes on in this town that I don't know. Doctor Hammond was an assistant surgeon years ago in the army, before he became a professor at the University of Maryland. With the war he rejoined the army at the very bottom of the list of assistant surgeons. It is no credit to the Army of the Potomac that they keep him in such a low position."

Sarah took the wine, thanked the woman, and went back to the wagon as the elegant carriage drew away. The way Mrs. Greenhow had recited the history of Doctor

Hammond seemed a bit strange. Almost as if she had memorized it. But then Sarah and Nubbin were taken with getting back to the hospital before the ice melted, and she forgot all about the woman.

That night the clouds finally broke. The rain came down in torrents, and Doctor Hammond had the nurses, who were all male, put on oilskins and scoop dirt out of the drains outside his tent hospital so the water wouldn't flow into the inside. When the wind blew with near the force of a hurricane, he was right there with them helping them to hold down the ropes and tent poles so the canvas wouldn't blow away and expose the sick soldiers to the elements.

About midnight the rain and wind stopped. The moon came out and fragments of clouds moved swiftly by to reveal the stars. Doctor Hammond made those who had worked outside get out of their wet clothing, wrap themselves in blankets, and take some of the chicken soup that had been made from two of the chickens brought back that afternoon.

Sarah busied herself visiting the men from the 2nd Michigan until the other young men who'd worked outside stepped behind some crates to shed their wet clothing, then strung it on ropes near the pot-bellied stove in the middle of the hospital. She waited so long that Doctor Hammond scolded her.

"Private Compton, you want typhoid?"

"No, Sir."

"Then get out of those wet clothes."

Sarah stepped behind the crates and wrapped some blankets around herself, bringing them up close under her chin. Doctor Hammond gave her a queer look. "It isn't that cold," he said. She took her soup and went to a corner to sit down by herself and eat it. It was very good.

CHAPTER SEVEN

July 4, The Same Hospital Tent in Washington

In the month that followed, Sarah and Nubbin made two trips a week into the heart of Washington to fetch food. Each time they brought back enough to keep the sick men in good supply. There would be no rancid butter or salt pork for Doctor Hammond's patients.

Once every week she went back to the camp of the 2nd Michigan to bring written reports from Doctor Hammond. Back at Camp Winfield Scott she'd stay the night in her tent, which she now had to herself. And relished the privacy. Back at the hospital she roomed with five other male nurses, although she'd managed to get around that, too, by offering to take night duty.

That way she got to sleep during the day. Alone in the quarters for male nurses.

In the month that followed, she wrote dozens of letters home for the sick men. She swept the floor of the hospital tent, and helped cook. Doctor Hammond had a special cook come in, a Negro woman from Washington whom everyone called simply Auntie Narcissa.

One day a ragged little Negro girl came into the tent to say that Auntie couldn't come that day. And so Doctor Hammond looked around at the nurses on day duty. "Can anybody here cook?" he asked. "We've fresh chickens. A soup will do for this evening."

Sarah knew she shouldn't, but she did. "I know some things from watching my ma," she said. "And my sisters."

He gestured to the stove. "Just throw everything in the pot," he told her.

The other male nurses in the hospital were all older than Sarah. And with the exception of Cowles, who was the orderly in charge of supplies because his father was a doctor, the others all seemed not quite right to Sarah. One seemed dim-witted. Another had more feminine mannerisms than her sister Betsy. The other three were clumsy with the patients, more often than not hurting them, and had become nurses, Sarah learned, to escape the possibilities of battle.

Every Saturday they cleaned. Under Doctor Hammond's direction, the floor was swept and scrubbed, and the bedclothes and men's garments were changed.

This was because on Sunday morning the head surgeon came to visit and inspect. He studied patient cards, prescribed drugs, examined and pronounced some ready to be returned to the field.

Every patient who was able to get out of bed and on his feet was made to stand beside his cot, no matter how weak. And salute the head surgeon, who came in dress uniform with a gleaming sword and attendants.

Sarah thought how stupid it was. Because they never saw this head surgeon other than Sunday mornings. And during the week Doctor Hammond did all the work, and, she strongly suspected, paid for some of the food she and Nubbin sometimes had to buy when donations weren't sufficient.

Twice in the month she was there, a supply of wine, pickles, canned sardines, and cake came delivered in a wagon. The crates were tagged with the name of Mrs. Rose Greenhow.

"Why is this woman sending us food?" Doctor

Hammond was angry. He'd summoned Sarah and Nubbin to him and they stood looking down at the crates.

"She stopped us once on the street, Sir," Sarah offered. "She's the one who sent that bottle of wine the first day I went out."

"Did she identify herself?"

"Yes, Sir."

"I told you not to take anything from anybody not on the list."

His scowl near brought her to tears. But tears were one thing that would betray her. Sarah had always known that. So she kept a stoic face. "You didn't say not to accept contributions, sir. She sent her compliments that day. She seemed to admire you."

He kicked one of the crates gently with his foot. "She's an unsavory character," he said. "Don't accept any more food from her."

"Sir?" Sarah was confused. She didn't think Doctor Hammond was a snob. Unsavory?

He scowled again. "Do you understand the King's English? I want nothing to do with that woman or her offerings. Enough said!"

"Yes, Sir," Sarah said. "Do we send these goods back then?"

"No. We keep them. But after this we send them back."

That night Sarah had some of the cake Mrs. Greenhow had sent and thought it the best she had ever tasted. Why did Doctor Hammond take exception to Mrs. Greenhow? She decided it was a romance gone sour and thought no more about it.

Sarah liked Doctor Hammond, though the other nurses grumbled about him. They thought him daft because he insisted all their drinking water first be boiled. And because the first week he made them all take a dose of "the bitters" every day. This was an ounce of whiskey with two grains of quinine.

"Necessary to ward off typhoid or malaria," he said. And he stood over them while they drank it.

The first time Sarah took it she had to run out of the tent to throw up.

He came out into the bright sunshine to stand beside her with a glass of water in one hand and a new glass of the bitters in the other. "I'd forgotten that some of you younger soldiers have never had whiskey," he said.

"I have," Sarah lied. "My daddy has his own still." Her father did not, of course, but it seemed the right thing to say. "Me and my brother Ben have tasted it since we were knee-babies. It's just that my stomach's empty, is all."

He gave her a queer look. "You're not coming down with the typhoid, are you?"

"No, Sir."

"Best let me examine you."

"No, Sir! I'm right well. Here, give me that, I'll take it right now again and show you how well I am." She took the glass of bitters and drank it down lickety-split, just to show him she could. Somehow she kept it down, though the whiskey burned her throat and made her shudder.

Next he made them all take the vaccination against smallpox.

Sarah became feverish, her limbs ached for two days afterward, and her neck became stiff. In turn, such effects overtook all the male nurses. And one afternoon, seeing Doctor Hammond examine Private Cowles, she knew that she could not permit herself to such or her secret would be found out. So she denied feeling poorly when Doctor Hammond asked.

"If it's all the same to you, Sir, I'd like to take this week's report back to the 2nd Michigan."

He signed it and she left the hospital. Back at Camp Winfield Scott she sought the privacy of her tent, where she was able to languish in her misery, unbothered for two days, until she felt better.

She had to get back and help plan tomorrow. They were putting on a musical for the soldiers in Doctor Hammond's tent. A special guest was coming, a man called the Comte de Paris, the son of the pretender to the crown of France. He was coming with a sketch artist from *Harper's*.

Sarah had decided that her contribution to the musical would be a rendering of a scene from *Uncle Tom's Cabin*, in which she had played Topsy. She knew the lines well. She had only to drape some homespun over herself, and, as she'd done back home, she would put burnt cork over her face and hands.

Three of the male nurses, including Cowles, sang. Another, named Bailey Snead, gave a reading from *David Copperfield*. Then Sarah did her heartrending monologue from *Uncle Tom's Cabin*.

The applause was loud and sustained. The entertainment was a success. Afterward, when she was serving cakes and coffee to the soldiers, the young man who called himself the Comte de Paris came up to her.

"I have never known a Negro," he said. "Is your depiction accurate?"

Sarah looked at the young man whom she considered vapid. On first meeting him she'd decided she'd die before she allowed herself to be called a pretender to anything. "I only know Nubbin, Sir. The little boy who helps around here. Otherwise, I only know what I've read. Why don't you ask that young man in the bed near the tent wall? He has relatives he visited before the war in South Carolina."

Sarah knew what answer the comte would get from young Jimmy Grimstead. And it gave her pure delight to send the comte to him. She watched in the candlelight as the comte leaned over Grimstead's bed to ask what the slaves were like on his people's plantation.

"Plantation?" the young Grimstead asked. And he propped himself up on his elbows. "Mr. Comte, my kin-folk don't live on no plantation with the white columns and the magnolias. They're dirt farmers. Country people. The slave owners, they're low-country. My kin got nary a slave on their place. They do all their own work. I never met a slave, no sir-ree."

"Then why are you fighting this war?" the comte asked.

"Because I hold with human dignity for all," Jimmy said.

The comte seemed disappointed. As he passed by Sarah he shrugged, then stopped to whisper something to her. "You have the gift of mimicry," he said. "I've a friend who will soon be in Washington who might like to meet you."

At best Sarah thought he was a fool.

July 10–15, The Same Hospital in Washington

In the July heat, Sarah felt an unreality about things. Sometimes, alone on duty at night with the crickets chirping outside and the sound of a harmonica from a distant camp, or the flash of heat lightning and rumble of thunder over the distant unfinished Capitol, she could not quite believe she had ever once lived on a farm in Michigan. She could not recall her mother's face. She felt as far removed from her growing-up years as if she had died and come back to life again in another time and place.

But she knew two things. And both worried her.

Her brother-in-law, her sister Clarice's husband, was with the latest group of men who'd come to join the 2nd Michigan. She'd seen him in Camp Winfield Scott her last trip there.

She knew she was going to have to have the mole on her face removed so he wouldn't recognize her. And soon.

The other thing that worried her was the rumor they'd soon be going into their first battle. She'd become fond of this hospital, Doctor Hammond, the other male nurses despite their peculiarities, Nubbin, with whom she made her twice-weekly trips for fresh food, and especially the men patients for whom she'd written letters and talked to in the night when they couldn't sleep.

Maybe she should have offered to be a nurse. But no, she'd come to fight and fight she would.

The next day she asked Doctor Hammond if he'd remove the mole from her face.

He was at the board table in the middle of the tent, writing. She brought him a cup of coffee. She knew he was working on a list of hospital reforms to be sent to the War Department. She hated bothering him. But she couldn't go back to Camp Winfield Scott with the mole on her face.

"Doctor Hammond?"

"Yes, Private?"

"I was wondering, Sir, if you could remove this mole I have on my face."

He set down his pen, accepted the cup of coffee she offered, and looked up at her. "Looks fine to me, Private Compton. Why do you wish it removed?"

She was ready with the answer. "Because some of the men back at camp have taken to calling me Frenchie. Because of the way French women paint moles on their faces to be in fashion. It's embarrassing, Sir."

He nodded. But his eyes, which were blue, and which went a sort of silver when he got thoughtful or angry, seemed like two slivers that had fallen from the moon as he looked at her.

"You don't have to go into battle if you don't want to, Compton," he said. "I'll write a request that you're indispensable to me here. I have some jurisdiction, you know."

Sarah looked at the floor. "Got nothing to do with going into battle, Sir."

"Doesn't it?"

"No, Sir. Why should it?"

He nodded. "All right, I can do it this afternoon. Is there anything you want to tell me, Compton?"

"Tell you, Sir? About the mole? I've had it since I was born."

"Not about the mole, Compton. Anything else. You can trust me. I promise."

Sarah had no idea what he was talking about. That afternoon he removed the mole, bandaged her face, and sent her back to camp with some laudanum. She was the only one of all the nurses going back. "I'll miss you," Doctor Hammond said. "Godspeed, Private Compton."

She had to turn away from him on going, for the tears in her eyes.

CHAPTER EIGHT

July 17, Camp Winfield Scott, Washington

TO SARAH IT WAS LIKE THE FOURTH OF JULY. ALL around her on the hills outside Washington could be heard the cheering of the soldiers, the patriotic songs, and the music of the regimental bands as the Army of the Potomac commenced its march to fight.

They'd been told it would be a two-day march and many of the 2nd Michigan had been given new shoes that morning. When she put them on, Sarah thought they were rather flimsy, and she didn't like the way they rubbed her heels. But they were new. The army was taking care of their own.

All around her as they marched away from Camp Winfield Scott she heard jubilant cries of "On to Richmond!" from the troops.

"We'll whip them this day!" came one cry.

And, "I'll be home for the fall harvest!"

Sarah was ready. Her canteen of water was full. Her cartridge box that hung on her waist belt held four pounds of ammunition. Across her back was her bedroll and in her haversack her hardtack and salted pork. The 2nd Michigan was in the main column and it was said they'd reach Fairfax by evening. As they marched one hour, then two, the day became hotter and hotter, and Sarah wished the long blue Union blouses they'd been issued were made of anything but wool. At home in the fields she'd have worn a muslin shirt on such a day, with the sleeves rolled up above her elbows. She was accustomed to the heat of the day. But in Virginia it seemed ten times worse than in Michigan.

She tried not to think about her thick woolen hose, or the fact that they weren't thick enough to keep her heels from being rubbed raw on the new shoes. As they marched and marched through the lush Virginia country-side, Sarah paid less mind to the scenery and more to the ground beneath her, which had some ruts and was so dusty she sometimes had to cough. Half an hour outside Camp Winfield Scott the troops stopped singing. The people who'd lined the road to cheer them were gone. And there was only the sound of the tramp, tramp, tramping of boots and shoes, the occasional neighing of a horse pulling the hospital wagons, and the mumble of complaints from the ranks.

When she thought she couldn't bear it anymore, when the straps that held her canteen and haversack cut into her shoulders and the weight of the cartridge box made her back ache, a sergeant called a halt for the night.

Soldiers all around her were dropping to the ground. Faces and necks were burned red and Sarah felt sorry for some boys who'd been clerks or students and had never had to abide the bite of the summer sun.

They made camp that night in Fairfax. Foragers were sent out for butter and milk and bread. Sarah heard cattle lowing in the distance. She drank the last of the boiled water Doctor Hammond had put in her canteen and went to the nearby stream for more. She heard shots fired in the distance and ran back to the camp for fear the enemy had sighted them.

"It's nothing," Colonel Fenton told them. "Our boys are getting some supper."

By dusk, fires glowed brightly in camp, shooting sparks into the warm darkness. Skewered on spits were parts of the cows that had been shot, chickens, even fish from the stream. There was an air of gaiety about the whole thing that made it feel like a picnic and Sarah went to sleep under the stars with a full stomach and the sound of singing in the distance.

But then, in what seemed like only an hour Colonel Fenton shook her awake and she heard reveille beat. All around her men were up, gathering their things, dark forms in a dream. Was it morning already? Overhead she saw some stars and the crescent moon was still visible. Some fires still burned and she smelled coffee and bacon, saw some soldiers making hoe cakes. Her mouth tasted like she'd just eaten a scorched porcupine. She needed to relieve herself.

"On your feet, Soldier." She felt a gentle boot in her thigh. "We march immediately."

"No breakfast?" came a cracked young voice from nearby.

"Didn't you eat enough last night, son? If we get marching we can get two or three hours in before the sun gets high. We lost a number yesterday from sunstroke."

Somehow, order was gotten out of the chaos and they were on the march again. As the sun rose in the east, squinting at them, some of the young men from the 2nd Michigan fell out of line to fill their canteens at the creek, others to pick blackberries along the way. The officers on horseback were everywhere, shouting commands, herding them back, even wielding swords.

They could not keep the men in line. They did not know how to keep in line thousands of young men who, like Sarah, were away from home for the first time and marching to battle and maybe even to death.

As the day wore on, Sarah found herself thinking about the death part. She did not worry the matter. She could shoot. Hadn't she shot off Zeke Kunkle's hat from two hundred yards?

By late afternoon Sarah's head was throbbing. Her body itched from the woolen trousers and shirt. Her feet ached and when she looked down she could see the soles separating from her shoes.

Ahead of her some soldiers were already tripping over their disintegrating shoes and cussing.

They passed a stone church. Somebody said they were in Centerville. Up ahead Sarah saw General McDowell, the head of the army, talking on horseback with two other officers. The troops marched for what seemed like another half hour, then collapsed on the ground. Sarah knew she had to set up her tent, but she was too weary to even think about doing it. She rolled under a tree, her head bursting. Then she felt the point of a sword in her side.

"On your feet, Soldier." She looked up. Backlit by the evening sun was General McDowell. Sarah bolted to her feet. "Yes, Sir."

"Set up your tent and get a good night's rest. We fight tomorrow." His voice gentled, and Sarah obeyed.

They were short of rations, and there was no foraging. Somebody said the enemy was just over the hills. Sarah wondered what they looked like. She had never seen a Rebel soldier. She wondered if she could really shoot another human being. That night she wandered the camp by the firelight. So many boys were writing home. She wanted to, but couldn't.

She wandered to the edge of a camp Meeting. Men were praying. The mood was somber now. Sarah lingered a while listening to them respectfully. Somebody said something about the throne of grace. Somebody else about being a faithful soldier of Jesus. And Sarah thought that if Jesus was in charge here He'd see to it that they at least had loaves and fishes to eat. Then she thought that was like blasphemy. They started praying, the same prayers her father prayed when he gathered the family together at night. After maybe knocking Sarah to the ground for not mending a fence right, and while her mother sat next to him with a swollen eye because she'd tried to stop him.

Sarah couldn't say such prayers. And she knew no others. So she said none at all, but walked slowly back to her tent, passing knots of men hunched over, talking in low whispers, some reading their Bibles. She had no friends here and she envied these young men. She even wished, that night, that she had a tentmate, but Cowles had stayed behind to help Doctor Hammond with the many wounded that would come in after the battle.

Sunday, July 21, Manassas, Virginia

As they marched Sunday morning before dawn, the first thing that struck Sarah was how pretty they looked up ahead, the Army of the Potomac, column after column of them, in the middle of the green hills. Then she heard the deep rumbling of artillery in the distance, like some beast up ahead. The others heard it too, but nobody said anything much. There was no joking now, no complaining, just the steady tramping of feet. Up ahead the road branched in three directions. She saw the troops being divided, the officers standing at the turnoffs, directing them with swords. The sun was up now and of a sudden Sarah could see the enemy.

They were on heights of earthworks a good distance away. The earthworks and fields seemed covered with Confederate infantry and artillery. She saw flags, horses, wagons, cannons. They formed up, taking their assigned places, an officer riding up and down behind their line telling them to "hold steady, boys. If you lose this today they can take Washington."

Then, from the enemy came a fearful explosion of shells, grape, and musketry. Men were falling all around Sarah. Instinctively, she dropped to the ground. Beneath her the ground trembled and she heard the terrible whooshing and explosion of shells.

Now all she could see was smoke from the enemy fire and all she could hear were cheers and yelling from across the space between them. Men were moaning around her. For what seemed a terrible length of time, the enemy continued firing. Shells screamed and exploded over and around them. The noise was deafening and Sarah felt a primitive urge to dig into the earth and hide.

She was aware of the officers on horses riding up and down. Then the brigade bugle sounded the charge. Around her the men got on their feet, Sarah with them, charging forward.

Blindly she followed the blue-coated figures in front of her, stepping over those who fell, even tripping and falling over them. Ahead were the earthworks filled with Rebels. Above, the sky vomited fire and smoke. Below her she slipped and skidded on blood, jumped over abandoned guns, blankets, haversacks, and canteens.

At one point they came behind a natural barrier of trees. Sarah saw her companions kneeling and readying to fire, so she did, too. She readied her musket. Then there was a click, click, clicking and spurts of flame all up and down the line, and they were moving forward. Up ahead there were rolling waves of flame from the Rebel cannon and their ranks seemed to break as the Union men kept firing and firing. Her regiment was running again, so Sarah ran with them. Running meant you were gaining ground. She felt, rather than saw, some cavalry dashing across the ground up ahead, saw the beautiful green earth churned up and parts of it blown through the air as a cannonball found its mark.

Then one of the Rebel cavalry officers on horseback was coming right at them. Sarah stopped, knelt on one knee, aimed Fanny, and fired.

The cavalry officer went down with his horse. There was the sound of the horse's terror, more guns going off around her, and men and horses screaming. And smoke. Such smoke.

Sarah saw the cavalry officer's horse get on its feet and

gallop toward her. She moved out of the way as the horse went by, eyes filled with fear, stirrups flapping.

The smoke cleared a bit, and men were running past her. The officer she'd shot was on the ground, gray coat and mustard-colored sash stained with blood. Sarah scrambled toward him.

He was groaning. "Water," he said, "give me some water." He could scarcely speak.

Sarah was aware of her fellow soldiers running by. She knelt, opened her canteen, and was about to offer it to him when she saw that his chest was torn apart. The breastbone was protruding.

Sarah paused, canteen in hand, feeling as if she'd been hit in the head.

She could see his heart, exposed and beating.

A dizziness came over her. She had done this! She must give him water. She guided the canteen to his lips, but they did not move. He was dead. Looking, she saw the heart was no longer beating.

Sarah turned away from the terrible spectacle and vomited on the ground. For a moment she felt her own heart exposed. Her whole being felt raw and used up. Then an officer came along and tapped her gently with the flat of his sword. "Come on, son, there's nothing you can do here but get shot."

Sarah took a drink of water to clear her mouth, covered her canteen, and got to her feet to continue on.

The sun was unmercifully hot now. Men were shedding their haversacks, blankets, and even their canteens. Far ahead of her she saw her regiment and knew she must catch up with them. The Rebel batteries had ceased firing for the moment and she knew she must take advantage of this lull. But the Reb soldiers were still coming. In the half hour or so that followed she reloaded Fanny what seemed like dozens of times as they moved forward. If she hit anyone else, she did not know. She did not look anymore, nor did she stop. She fell, got up, and fell again. Twice the Union men drove the Rebels off their fortifications and over the hill. But, like fire ants, they came back again, appearing and reappearing. And on their return, their artillery was more fierce than before.

Once she lost consciousness and awoke to hear the fighting farther away. She scrambled to her feet, found her hat, and ran to catch up with the nearest group of blue-clad soldiers.

They were firing up the hill. There was a house on the hill. Sarah saw a stone well nearby, a flower bed, some apple trees. She knelt down next to one of the soldiers. He looked at her.

"1st Rhode Island," he said.

"2nd Michigan," Sarah returned. "Got separated from my brigade."

He took aim and fired. "Join right in. That's the 8th Georgia up there."

Right after he fired, Sarah saw a man drop from one of the apple trees. Then their batteries fired and more men dropped from the trees.

"Like shot bears," a man nearby shouted gleefully.

"They say there's an old lady in that house," the Rhode Islander told Sarah as he took aim again. "She won't leave. About eighty-five, they say."

Then he fired, but Sarah couldn't hear the report, because over their heads the Rhode Island batteries fired, blowing the roof off the house.

The Rebs on the hill returned fire, a steady stream of it. Sarah saw the Rhode Islander open his mouth to say something to her. He was pointing to her left. She looked and saw the hill sloping away to some trees. She looked back at him. But he was gone. Blown away, his body flying through the air. The repercussion from the blast bowled Sarah over and she lost her footing and began to roll down the hill toward the trees.

The last thing she thought of before she lost consciousness was the eighty-five-year-old lady in the house at the top of the hill, whose roof had just been blown off.

CHAPTER NINE

July 21, Late night, Manassas, Virginia

THE RAIN WOKE SARAH. AT FIRST IT SEEMED LIKE A balm, warm and comforting, and just before gaining consciousness she thought she was home in the fields and thought how good the rain would be for the corn.

When she opened her eyes, it was dark and from somewhere in the distance she heard the moans of men and the sound of someone praying. She was aware, as she sat up, of a sticky wetness on her head and when she put her hand to her face it was scratched and raw. Her head throbbed.

Then she remembered. She'd hit it on the side of a tree after rolling down the hill.

Fanny, she thought, where was Fanny? She crept around on her knees in the wet grass until her hands came upon the barrel of the Winchester, then she sat back deciding what to do.

She did not know where she was. Or where she should be. She'd remembered the man from Rhode Island, the woman who wouldn't leave her house. What had happened to them?

On top of the hill she could see the broken outline of the house, smell the charred ruins. The whole top floor had been blown away and was still smoldering in the rain. Two chimneys, one at each end, pointed angrily to the heavens, accusing God.

The smell of burned ruins and the rotten-egg smell of musket fire lingered all around. In the distance, through the smoke that cloaked everything, she could see low ground fires and dead forms on the ground, as well as darkened images creeping over them and disappearing into the night. A horse nickered somewhere. She heard the creaking of wagon wheels and someone shout, "Over here! This one's alive." The drawl was Rebel.

Sarah got to her feet. She checked for her possessions. All were intact. Her clothing was already soaked through, and each movement she attempted made her head throb. But she knew she could not stay here. The battle must be over, since there was no more shooting. Who had won? It did not seem to matter. All that mattered now was that she find her people, her place.

All that mattered was that she be away from here, this nightmare scene, away from the moans, the smoke, the destruction. She moved forward.

In the dark, unsure of her footing, she tripped over canteens, rifles, even bodies. Or parts of bodies. She walked around one man who lay facedown, drowned in his own pool of blood. She stepped in blood and her shoes were so torn that she felt it seep through her socks and between her toes. Then, mercifully, she heard water. There was a stream nearby. She let its sound lead her down a slope. The gurgling water brought some measure of sanity. She put her hands in it, filled her canteen. She took off her shoes and dipped her feet in it. Then she washed the blood off her scratched face. She put her wet socks and torn shoes back on and when she stood up she was cold. So she took her blanket from her back, unrolled it, wrapped it around her and followed the stream for a bit, hoping she was going the right way.

Then she minded that she was down the slope from a road, and on the road, backlit by smoke and fires, were wagons. Ambulance wagons, she thought. They were piled with men. She heard the voices. She saw a woman riding astride with about fifteen canteens hanging from the pommel of her saddle. Sarah heard her say, "The stone church, we'll put them in there."

It was a Yankee voice. She went up the slope.

For the next hour she found herself part of the confusion on the main road back to Centerville, pushing her way through wagons piled with wounded. A squad of cavalry came through, mud-splattered, eyes dull, coats bloodied. One man's arm hung, half off. He leaned in agony over his horse's neck and went on past her.

The rain poured down. The road became muddy. Sarah tripped and fell once, but had to get up for fear of being run down by an ambulance wagon. But then she came upon a woman sitting in the middle of the road. "You must get out of the way," Sarah told her. "You'll be run down by the returning army."

"I don't know anything about the army," the woman told her. "I am cooking my husband's supper. Can't you see? You are in my way. My chicken is frying and it will burn."

Demented, Sarah thought. What is she doing here, anyway? Was she one of those "daughters of the regiment" she'd heard about? Women who followed their men into battle because they couldn't bear to be left home alone?

"You'll be killed if you stay here," Sarah insisted. "Come, get out of the road."

"This is my stove!" the woman insisted. Her eyes, when she looked at Sarah, seemed crossed. Not seeing.

"Well, come then, I'll help you move your stove out of the way," Sarah offered.

The woman submitted to this. And Sarah found herself making like she was moving a stove, with her on one end and the demented woman on the other, until they reached the side of the road. If anybody sees me they'll put me in the madhouse, Sarah thought. But then, perhaps it's where I belong for being here in the first place. Who is to say tonight who is mad and who is sane?

She left the woman at the side of the road, cooking chicken for her husband, who was likely the dead fellow who'd drowned in his own blood back at the battle scene. She went on.

Before long she came to a farmhouse. All about, under the ghastly light of pine-knot torches, she saw Rebel wounded. She saw women and men hurrying in and out, attending to them, and continued on. From inside the outbuildings of the farm came a hellish light and screams of the wounded and dying.

For a moment, standing in the drizzling rain and the mud, Sarah found herself crying. She was alone, despite the crowds pushing past her to make their way back to Washington. She was hungry and shivering cold. She did not know where to go, what to do. Her head pounded, her feet were in shoes that were near worthless. She wanted to sit down in the middle of the road with that poor demented woman she'd met, and pretend she was at home cooking chicken.

It was easier than this.

Unknowingly, she sank to her knees. But before she was there a minute a soldier came by. "Get on with you, lad. You can't stop now. Keep on. It's only twenty-two miles to Alexandria."

He helped her to her feet.

As he did, Sarah saw that his blouse was shot away and his shoulder had a gaping wound. She felt ashamed. She should have been helping him. She went on.

At what must have been near midnight she came upon a fire burning in the yard of a farmhouse. It was under a tree, somewhat protected from the rain. Lights glowed in the farmhouse and she saw people bringing more wounded inside. Sarah was so exhausted she walked into the yard, toward the fire.

Around it were a number of men, disheveled and eating

the last of the contents of their tin cups. "Cornmeal gruel," one of them said. "Go behind the house and they'll give you some. It's right good."

They were Rebels. But they didn't seem to mind that she wasn't. Sarah fished for her own tin cup and went round to the back of the house where some women were giving out the mush. They ladeled it into her cup, she thanked them and went back to the fire and stood behind the men. Looking up at her, the one who had directed her to the gruel motioned she take her place, so she did, between him and the one who had a bandage over half his head.

They sat with their feet to the fire in silence. Looking around, Sarah determined that most of them were wounded. In the face, the arms, the legs. Nobody looked at her. By now Sarah's teeth were chattering and she ate the gruel gratefully. On either side of her the two men lay down on the ground, wrapping their blankets around them. By the time Sarah finished her gruel, all the others had, too. So she did likewise, lying between the two men for warmth.

Monday, July 22, Somewhere Outside Washington

When she awoke the rain was still coming down, but it was daylight. Stiffly, she sat up, her head aching. All the men around the fire were gone, with the exception of the two on either side of her. And they weren't stirring. Sarah looked down at each of them in turn, then touched them.

Their faces were cold. They had no pulse. They had died during the night.

She had slept between two dead men!

She jumped up. The smell of coffee came from the back of the house. She stumbled over there. The women were so busy they didn't bother even looking in her face as they poured coffee into her cup and broke off a piece of cornbread for her. "There's two men dead by the fire," she told them. They nodded, thanked her, and kept giving out coffee. Sarah walked away, eating and drinking the hot, bitter coffee, which tasted like a heavenly brew.

All day she went on, over muddy roads. Had they won? Not likely, she decided, else why would the Rebels still be in the area. No one who passed her could say. If they hadn't, would the Rebels be in Washington? She didn't dare ask the question. She went on. Over fences, through house lots. She saw a sign that told her she was on Fairfax Road. Beside it a man was slumped, moaning, gesturing to her. Sarah went to him. He was missing a leg.

"Water," he begged.

Sarah took her canteen and held it to his lips. He was young and fine-looking, but for the missing leg. "I'm from

Massachusetts," he said. In one hand he held a gold locket. "Will you get this to my wife?"

Sarah took the locket. Inside was the likeness of a comely young woman holding a baby on her lap. On the other side of the locket was printed her name and address. Lowell, Massachusetts, it said.

Sarah looked down at him. He seemed to swoon, then recovered. "Please get it to my wife. And tell her I love her. Always. Will you do that for me, son?"

Sarah promised she would. "But let me help you to one of the wagons. They come along every so often," she said.

"No, go along. The Rebs may be coming. You don't want to be a prisoner. We've lost this battle but there will be others. I'm dying. Go."

Sarah looked down the road, into the slashing rain. She heard horses' hooves. "Could be Reb cavalry," the man said. "Go!"

Sarah went, crying, the locket clutched in her hand.

Sometimes she stopped and hid when horses came by. Once she hid on the lee side of a stone well. Another time behind a tree. That time she dozed, snuggled in her wet blanket, holding hard onto Fanny, dreaming she was in her brother Ben's bedroom again, holding Fanny and peering out to look for Ezekiel Kunkle.

She'd hear tramping feet and wait for the men to walk by and follow on the road. Then the gray turned into the dark. Another night. She would walk all night, she decided. No more fires, no more sleeping between dead men for her. She was not alone on the road, however. Ambulance wagons passed. Batteries pulled by horses. Lone men and men in clusters, like people out of a dream, all making for Alexandria or Washington.

Sarah stopped a few times during the night to rest. But by the time the spires of Washington appeared in the distance in the unpromising gray light of morning she felt new strength and hurried on. She would go back to Camp Winfield Scott, she decided. She would see if anything was left of anything.

CHAPTER TEN

July 31, Washington

IT WAS STILL RAINING. SARAH TURNED OVER IN HER damp bedroll in her tent back at Camp Winfield Scott. A crack of thunder had wakened her. No, it was something else. Someone was singing. Several someones. She sat up.

It was a hymn, long, mournful, and haunting. Sarah crept out of the tent. All she saw, at first, was rain, a few sputtering fires, and in the distance, pickets.

Then she saw them. A crowd of people, well over a

dozen, were huddled at the end of the line of tents, and she saw Colonel Fenton and two aides with them.

Automatically she reached for Fanny and, shoeless, her feet squishing on the muddy ground, she approached them.

They were Negroes, soaking wet, wearing ragged linsey-woolsey clothing, many without shoes. They wore old floppy hats, torn bits of burlap, soaked blankets. One by one, Sarah was joined by soldiers who came out of their tents to see about the commotion.

For a while everyone, including Colonel Fenton, just stood and watched them. Some of them were shouting, some praying, some singing and some speaking. Then Colonel Fenton held up his hand and they went quiet.

"I 'members the first time I see the Yankees comin'" one woman was saying, "They come gallopin' down the road, jumpin' over the fence, tromplin' down the bushes an' messin' up the flower beds. They stomped all over the house, in the kitchen, pantries, smokehouses an' everything. I was settin' on the steps when a big Yankee man come up. Glory be, I say, glory to the Lord!"

There was more shouting. And praying to the Lord. Then Colonel Fenton shouted. "Where do you all come from?"

"We'uns come from Fortress Monroe," one large Negro man said. "These others, we meet on the road comin' here.

We'uns heared 'bout the firin' on Sumter. We run'd to Fortress Monroe. There we meet Gen'l Butler. Our master come after us, but bless that gen'l man, he say no, we ain't goin' back. Bless that man! He call us contraband."

Another black hand went up in the back of the crowd. "Our master was gettin' us ready to sell south, lessin' we escape when the war come. We ran. We see the flag, Master, that flag you flyin' over there. We see it over the river. An' we keep headin' to the flag. An' we come here."

An elderly black man, old beyond years, with a white beard, took off his dripping, floppy hat. "I tell you, my breddern, that the good Lord has borne with this here slavery a long time with great patience. But now he can't bore it no longer, nohow; and he has said to the people of the North — go an' tell the slaveholders to let the people go, that they may serve Me. Now we wants to be here, on this sacred ground, under this flag. We serve you. We do what you need to win this war against the slavers. When the picket guard let us through, we kneel down an' kiss the ground. You gonna let us stay?"

"All right, all right," Colonel Fenton said. "You can stay here the night. We have some extra tents since we lost a goodly number of our men in the battle. Then we'll find out where to put you. Sergeant Kelly!" he shouted. "Build up this fire. Put a camp kettle on. Get some bread and meat. These people are starving! Come on, boys, can't you see? These people are starving!"

"Yes, Master," the old Negro with the white beard said. "We's hungry arright. We been on the road fer two days and we ain't had nothin' but berries."

Sarah put Fanny aside and, with the others, set herself to the task of helping. She led some of the women and children to the empty tents. She found extra, dry blankets, food, hot coffee. For most of that night she and her fellow soldiers stayed up, drinking coffee with the slaves, and listening to their stories. Sarah had heard so much about slavery, had tried to imagine so many times what it must be like, not only to be Negro but to be held in bondage. Yes, she had known and spoken with Nubbin, but he was a child, still carefree and unaware of the terrible tragedy being played out among his elders. On the plantation he'd come from he'd told her he played with the white children. Sarah realized, speaking with the escaped slaves that night, that she had never really met or spoken in depth with a Negro person before.

It rained for two days after the battle, which the Union had lost, and then the sun came out with a vengeance. The feeling in camp over the lost battle was disbelief and discouragement. Sarah worried. Her brother-in-law, Tobias, was not in camp, had not returned from the battle. Sarah spent her spare time going around asking after him. But no one had seen him since the fight. And no one cared. Tobias had always been an oddment where people were concerned. And in the army he'd made no friends. Besides, everyone was exhausted from drilling.

A new commander-in-chief had been appointed. His name was General George McClellan. Word ran through camp. He was only thirty-two. A West Point graduate.

By the sixth day of drilling, Sarah's legs and feet ached. They'd been given new shoes and Colonel Fenton was writing to somebody named Allan Pinkerton who ran a new secret service for General McClellan, to complain about the shoddy shoes given his soldiers.

"Some Boston merchant cheated us," she heard Fenton say, dictating his letter to his aide. "No wonder the Rebels hate us."

Sarah's face was now green and purple on the left side, with several scratch marks that were puffy and red. Her face hurt when she lay down at night, but she'd been almost glad of the pain, for every time she closed her eyes to sleep she saw, in flashes, the face and bloody, torn-apart chest of the Confederate cavalry officer she'd shot.

She wondered who he was, who was at home waiting for him.

Two days after the battle she wrote to Mrs. Constance Beckett of Lowell, Massachusetts. "I have your locket," she wrote, after telling how she'd been with Mrs. Beckett's husband when he died. "When circumstances permit, I shall send it to you in a proper package."

Writing the letter helped some, but she found herself wishing she knew the name and address of the Confederate officer. If she did, she'd write to his wife, too, she told herself. Then she wondered if that would be treason. And she knew she should be writing to Clarice.

A week after the battle Colonel Fenton told her to report again to Doctor Hammond. She was so happy she could have kissed the colonel. She needed to get away from the stultifying disappointment at their losses, in camp. And maybe Doctor Hammond knew something about Tobias.

The tent hospital was overflowing with wounded from the battle. There weren't enough cots, so bedding had been placed on the floor. Some men were even on the ground outside, under the trees now that the rain had stopped. There weren't enough blankets, either, or medical supplies. Water was a big problem, and Doctor Hammond had his nurses constantly boiling water on the stove, which made the room hot and steamy.

Before she went into the main tent, Sarah peeked into

the operating room tent. It was empty now, and a few flies buzzed in spite of the scrubbed cleanliness of the empty table and wooden floor. As she approached the main tent, she heard the moans of some men, but nothing prepared her for what she saw inside.

So many men were amputees, missing arms and legs. Others wore splints or had half their faces bandaged. One or two were trying to make it about on crutches. Those who were sleeping tossed and turned and cried out in their dreams.

Doctor Hammond was at the table in the middle of the tent. He lifted eyes that were heavy with discouragement and weariness to Sarah when she reported. "That's some bruise you've sustained," he said. "You didn't go hand to hand with a Reb, did you?"

"No, Sir, I rolled down a hill and hit my face on a tree."

Immediately, he stood up and put his hands on either side of her face. His touch was gentle. He peered into her eyes. "Any headaches or vomiting?"

"No, Sir, I'm fine."

"Any other wounds?"

"Just my feet, Sir. The shoes wore out before we got there. But I was given some salve back at camp, and if not for the drilling, I'd be fine."

"Yes. I know. Drill, drill, drill. I've had a dozen new

sunstroke cases from it. Well, McClellan's bound to bring the army to some kind of new discipline. I've known him for a while. And he's as dedicated as I am to sanitation. We're swamped with new cases, as are all the hospitals in Washington, as well as Alexandria, Georgetown, and Bull Run. Lots of these cases are measles, pneumonia, and dysentery. I heard the 2nd Michigan lost a dozen souls."

"Yes, Sir. Have you heard anything about a Tobias Munday?"

"No. Why?"

"I knew him from back home. He's missing since the battle."

"So are lots of others. I'll keep an eye open for his name. I was at the battle." He gave a bitter laugh. "I had a notebook with me. I intended to make a list of the killed and wounded. I saw near a hundred dead before I came upon one wounded. Needless to say, I gave up on that idea fast." He sat down and shook his head. "A thirty-day war, they all said. We're lucky if it's over in thirty months. We're short of food, supplies. I'm out of morphine already. I've got to find a volunteer to take a trip five miles into Virginia. There's a doctor's house just across the Potomac. I heard on the field that he was killed outright. Tom Briscoe. He had two sons in the battle also. I don't know how they fared. But I do know his wife has got a supply of morphine and other things I badly need."

"Is that why you summoned me, Sir? I'd be glad to go," Sarah said.

He looked up at her. "Good Lord, no. I was thinking of sending one of the nurses."

"I can ride just as good as they can. Maybe better. And I'm more than a fair hand with a gun," Sarah told him.

For some reason, sending her hadn't occurred to him. He shook his head, as if to right his thoughts. "I'd have to get permission from your commanding officer. Anyway, I need you to go with Nubbin and get me more food this afternoon. We need it more than ever."

"I'd be glad to, Sir. You could sent the note to Colonel Fenton while I'm gone. And if he says yes, I could go tonight. Wouldn't it be better traveling at night anyway?"

Again he gave her a look, this time of astonished respect. "Sometimes I think you should be more than a private, Compton. All right then, go find Nubbin. He's hitching up the mule. I'll send the note while you're gone."

"Could I ask a favor first?"

"Certainly."

Sarah drew the locket out of her pocket and set it down on the board table. "The address is inside. I've already written to Mrs. Beckett. But I was wondering if you could wrap the locket up proper-like and send it back to her."

His eyes softened as he took the locket, opened it, stared at it for a moment, then looked up at Sarah. "Did you know her husband, Private Compton?"

Of a sudden, Sarah found she could scarce control her voice. "No, Sir. I came upon him when he was dying. He gave the locket to me. I came upon others, too, on the way back. One was a Confederate officer I shot."

Some understanding came across Doctor Hammond's brown eyes, like the sun on a cloudy day. "I see. And this man you shot. He, too, died?"

"He was dying, sir. I saw," Sarah hesitated. "His chest was shot open. I saw his heart beating."

He nodded. "A harsh sight for a young farm boy from Michigan." His voice seemed edged with something Sarah could not name. When he said the word "boy" there seemed to be a special emphasis on it. A thrill of fear went through her. Did he suspect? "But then, we are at war, Private," he continued briskly. "Unfortunately when you get that close it seems rather senseless. Different from running across a meadow with the flags flying and the drums beating, feeling part of something wonderful, isn't it?"

"Yes, Sir."

"Are you sorry you enlisted then?"

"Oh, no, Sir. I want to do my part."

"Well, today your part is fetching food with Nubbin. I'll send the locket," he said. Then, as she started to leave, "Oh, Private, one more thing."

"Yes, Sir?"

"Be careful on the streets of the city. There are contrabands and discouraged solders wandering everywhere. Some people are angry because we lost the battle. The saloons are overcrowded. Do your errands and return directly. Do you have a pistol on you?"

"No, Sir. I have Fanny."

"Fanny?"

"My Winchester, Sir."

He went to his coat, which was draped over a nearby chair. His uniform coat. He was a captain in rank. Sarah noticed how dirty and torn it was from the battle. Out of the pocket he took a pistol, checked to make sure it was loaded, and handed it to her. "It's a Remington," he said. "Can you manage it?"

"Yes, Sir." Sarah put it in her belt.

"Just showing it may help you if you're accosted. You may take it tonight, if Colonel Fenton gives permission." Then he turned and went back to his work.

And so it was that Sarah and Nubbin were in the

wagon again, making their way through the streets of Washington. But it was different now. Sarah saw the difference right off.

There were more fortifications being built, no matter which way you looked, for miles along the Potomac. And every few miles mounted cannons were on those fortifications. There were soldiers everywhere, marching. And on the streets, wagons filled with supplies and surrounded by outriders. They had to stop once for a parcel of horses being brought to the pens by the Washington Monument. And there were Negroes everywhere, just like the ones who'd come to Sarah's camp, wandering barefoot, carrying sacks of possessions, waiting in line for food as women dished out soup under a banner that said "Sanitary Commission."

They ran into a few rowdies who'd just come out of the bars, from which the sound of banjo music emanated. Once the rowdies stopped Sarah and Nubbin in the middle of the street. "One of our brave soldiers," one said. "Whip the Rebs in thirty days, hey? Well, what happened?"

Sarah didn't have to use the pistol. The man's fellow rowdies dragged him off, ashamed. She had more trouble with Nubbin, who begged her constantly to tell him about the battle.

Sarah did not want to talk about the battle. But finally she gave in. "What do you want to know?"

"How many Rebs you kill?"

She turned the conversation away from killing. She told him of the way the men had marched, though their shoes were worn to nothing, how the Rebels had lined up across the field, flags flying in the sun. She told him the good things. About the elegant and brave cavalry horses, the way the men at the batteries had manned their guns.

"But we lost," Nubbin reminded her woefully.

"We'll win next time," she promised.

"Did you kill anybody?"

Sarah lied. "No," she said.

"We best win. My pappy says he never go back to bein' a slave. Never." They rode on the wagon seat in silence for a while, then he spoke again. "'Ceptin', he warn't treated bad. None of us wuz. T'wasn't anythin' wrong about home that made us run. My pappy heard so much talk 'bout freedom, I reckon he jus' wanted to try it, and so he said we had to get away from home to have it."

"Do you miss home?" Sarah asked him.

"I miss Nancy and Tyler."

"Who are Nancy and Tyler? Family you left back in Virginia?"

"No," Nubbin said wistfully. "They be the white chillens I played wif.' We 'uns had us a hideout under the branches of the hemlock tree. Them branches hang down real low. We could watch everythin' that went on in front of the house from that hideout. I wonder if they miss me. You think they miss me, Private?"

"I think so," Sarah told him. "I think we all have things we miss by now."

They made their usual collections of food and all went well until they started for Sixteenth Street. Up ahead was the spire of St. John's Church. They were headed for the rectory, where the pastor's wife was always very generous with donations.

Just as they were starting down the pleasant street, which was not far from the President's house, three men in coats and bowler hats came toward them and held out their hands to halt the mule and wagon.

"Where are you two going?" one of the men asked. He wore a check coat that Sarah thought was ridiculous-looking. Nevertheless, he seemed important.

"I'm Private Neddy Compton of the 2nd Michigan," Sarah said. "On detached duty, working for Doctor Hammond. We're fetching food for the sick. And this," she gestured to Nubbin, "is my assistant. He works for Doctor Hammond, too."

The man in the ridiculous coat nodded. "I've heard of

Hammond. He's a friend of McClellan's. Still, I can't allow the wagon through this afternoon. We're conducting surveillance on this street. You have to turn back."

Before she did, Sarah took a good look down the street. In front of a three-story, pink-brick house with white shutters were gathered a number of men like this one.

"That be the house of the lady my ma sometimes works for who has all the parties," Nubbin whispered to her. "What do surveillance mean?"

"It means watching," Sarah explained. "They're watching her house."

"Why?" Nubbin asked.

"I don't know."

"Maybe those mens be jealous 'cause they ain't invited to her parties. My ma says she got a lot of men friends, that lady. Ain't she the one what give us the wine that day?"

Sarah said yes, she was, then told him they ought to start back to the hospital before the food began to spoil.

CHAPTER ELEVEN

August 2, Washington

IT WAS DARK WHEN SARAH LEFT FOR VIRGINIA THAT night. Colonel Fenton had given permission, but he and the doctor had argued, Hammond told her.

"He wanted you to go out of uniform. It would be safer to say you were a relative visiting to console her for her husband's death. But what would a young man be doing out of uniform in these times? If you were a girl it would be different."

Sarah said nothing. Just stood and waited, her heart beating wildly inside her chest. Doctor Hammond sat slumped in his chair, brooding. "Out of uniform would be safer, except if you were caught. Then you'd be shot as a spy. If you're caught in uniform you at least have this."

He handed her an official-looking piece of parchment. She read it quickly. It said she was on a mission under his direction. A mercy mission for supplies for the wounded.

"Sometimes the truth is the most simple and the best," he said. "Unless you run into the most hardened Reb, they'll let you through. Of course, you may not be caught at all. Pray God, that will be the case. Whatever happens, don't lose that paper. Or give it over to anyone."

With that promise Sarah took off. The horse she'd been given reminded her of Max, he was so lively and dear. Just riding a horse again gave her comfort, made her feel that nothing could hurt her. She had her map, also given her by Doctor Hammond. And she had no trouble on the Long Bridge that crossed the Potomac, though she was told there would be a guardhouse on the Rebel side.

There was. But the guard had a friend with him and fortunately they were still celebrating the South's victory at Manassas, for they were half in their cups. They read Doctor Hammond's letter with a cursory glance and, after asking how far she was going for supplies, told her to be back within two hours or they'd send someone hunting for her. Then they waved her through.

Sarah rode on through the darkening night. The air was silky and the earthy fragrance of the countryside, with the added smell of nearby cattle, made her feel at home. She felt she could ride on forever. But in no time at all, it seemed, she came upon the farmhouse, about three miles from the main road. There was a gate, and then a lane that led to the house.

It was a large house, two stories, with generous brick chimneys on either end. Oil lamps gleamed inside the curtained windows. And in the distance Sarah could see the cornfields. She felt a pang of homesickness. Lamplight, real rooms, farm smells. How she missed them all!

She dismounted in front and hitched the horse to a post, then used the large brass knocker on the door. The woman who answered was tall and thin and very dignified. She wore her hair knotted under a net in back, and her dress was black, as was appropriate to mourning.

"To what fortunate circumstances am I to attribute the pleasure of this unexpected call?" she asked.

She did not look as if anything was a pleasure to her. Sarah decided it was sarcasm. "I'm the courier for Doctor

Hammond at a Washington hospital," she explained. "He's badly in need of supplies. He knew your husband, and said you would help us."

A shadow seemed to cross the delicate features. "Ah, yes, Doctor Hammond," she said. "Do come in."

Sarah wiped her shoes on the mat before entering. "Let me extend my condolences for your loss, Ma'am. Doctor Hammond sends his compliments."

"Yes. He once worked under my husband's guidance." She ushered Sarah into a small parlor where Sarah gave her the list of supplies needed.

"I must be back within the hour or the guards at the Long Bridge will send soldiers out looking for me," she said.

The woman seemed nervous. She started out of the room, stopped, glanced at Sarah, then to some middle distance behind her, then started out of the room again. "I'll get directly to this. I was just having some tea. Help yourself." She indicated a silver tray on a table.

Sarah was not accustomed to such elegance. The silk draperies on the windows, the Persian carpet on the floor, the profusion of books in glass-fronted cases, the ticking of a tall clock, not to mention the silver tray and china cups, flooded her with yearnings she could not put a name to. They had no such luxuries at home, and her surroundings lulled her. She picked up a newspaper from Richmond and started reading accounts of the recent battle.

Then she wondered how this woman managed to live in Rebel country when her husband and sons were fighting for the Yankees. She supposed it was because he'd been a doctor.

She drank her tea and leaned back in the rocker. Fifteen minutes went by. The clock struck the quarter hour, fifteen minutes past eleven.

Sarah stood up, set her cup down, and ventured into the center hall. "Ma'am?"

There was a winding staircase that led to the upper floor. The banister was of thick polished wood. Above, on the landing, were oil paintings of people of the last century. Sarah decided that either Mrs. Briscoe or her husband belonged to one of the first families of Virginia.

"Yes?" came the reply from above stairs.

"I haven't much time. I must soon be starting back."

"You must understand," came the muffled answer. "It's difficult, going through my husband's things."

Sarah sighed and went to sit back down. The clock chimed another quarter of an hour. Surely it couldn't take so long to get together the necessary items! She was getting suspicious. Did she hear voices upstairs? But, of course, the woman had servants. She could not possibly be alone in this house.

Still Sarah betook herself once again to the hall. "Ma'am?" she called up the stairs.

The woman started to come down. In her hands was a basket. As she reached the end of the stairway she headed into the kitchen. "I want to send back some butter and eggs with you," she called over her shoulder.

"Please don't detain me any longer," Sarah begged.

She came out of the kitchen with another basket, a small one covered with a napkin. Her face was very white, Sarah noticed, and she seemed to be trembling.

"Mrs. Briscoe, I'm sorry if fetching your husband's things was painful for you," Sarah said. "Are you all right?"

"I'm perfectly fine." She walked Sarah to the front door.

Before Sarah went out she held out a greenback, as Doctor Hammond had directed.

"Oh, it is of no consequence," the woman said. "I am glad to contribute."

Sarah thanked her, took the two baskets, and went out. "I'll have to put the things in my saddlebags. I can't haul baskets. I'll leave them at the hitching post," she said. And she proceeded to do so, carefully packing the medicines, lint, and food into her saddlebags. Then, as she turned to set the two baskets down on the walk near the hitching post and was about to mount her horse, she heard the discharge of a pistol.

The report was so loud and unexpected that all Sarah could do at first was drop to the ground and hold her hand in front of her face. She felt the bullet whiz by. "What the devil," she yelled. Then she reached for her own pistol, but Mrs. Briscoe was in the act of firing again. Sarah held her pistol firmly. Was the woman mad?

Another report from Mrs. Briscoe's gun. The bullet whizzed far to the right of Sarah's ear.

Sarah fired back, determined not to kill her, but to frighten her. Mrs. Briscoe's pistol went flying and she screamed and held up both hands.

Sarah could see that one dripped blood. The woman was shrieking wildly. "You tried to kill me! And I lost a husband and two sons in the battle! I have no one, and you, a Yankee soldier, come here and try to kill me." She was crying hysterically.

Sarah put her pistol in her belt and went to Mrs. Briscoe, who was now on the ground, moaning. There seemed to be a terrible lot of blood. Quickly, she untied the end of her halter strap and wound it around the wrist of the woman's wounded hand. She wished she had hot salty water to purify the wound, soot from the fireplace to press against the cut, any of the remedies her mother had taught her. She satisfied herself by rummaging in the saddlebags for some clean lint and bandaging the hand.

When that was done she helped the woman to her feet, but she held on to the end of the halter strap. "Let me go!" Mrs. Briscoe seemed crazed. Her neat hairdo had come undone. She was pulling away. From the upper floors of the house, Sarah saw some gas lamps lit. Fear coursed through her. If the servants perceived trouble they'd call for help. She'd never get out of Rebel territory!

She drew her pistol again, at the same time pulling the woman out of the light that splashed onto the ground from the upper windows, one of which now opened.

"Mrs. Briscoe! You arright, Ma'am? Was that gunfire?" The voice was that of a Negro servant. Sarah saw him leaning out the window. She held the gun to the woman's side.

"Say yes," she whispered savagely. "Say some soldiers just went by."

"I'm fine, Pompey," Mrs. Briscoe called out. "I'm going for a stroll in my garden. Some soldiers just went by. They must be drunk."

The window shut, and in a minute or so the gas-lit lamp moved away.

"You bring an alarm and I'll have the whole countryside of Rebs down on me," Sarah whispered in the woman's ear. "Now I have to get back across the river. I'm taking you with me."

"You have no right!"

"I have every right. And duty. I don't know why you tried to shoot me. I'm not the enemy!"

"You are!" They were whispering at each other viciously now.

All the while, Sarah was pulling her over to her horse. "Oh? And tell me how that came to be?"

"All of you are. This war." The sobbing picked up in pitch again. "All you soldiers are to blame. We had a good life here. Now I have nothing."

Sarah mounted her horse. "Get on behind me."

"I won't."

"Get on, I said. If you don't you'll walk. Or more likely be dragged behind."

With another sob, the woman obeyed. Sarah helped pull her up behind her, surprised at how light in weight she was. Then she drew the woman's hands around her, and tied them in front of her uniform blouse.

For almost five miles as they made their way along darkened roads in the night, Mrs. Briscoe gave Sarah the rough side of her tongue. "Crazy," she'd say, "you're all crazy, all the army. Both the armies. I've lost everything. I hate all soldiers."

"You just behave yourself when we get to the guard post at the bridge," Sarah threatened, "or when we get to Union lines I'll tell them you're a Rebel spy."

As they got closer to the Long Bridge, Mrs. Briscoe's tongue turned softer. Her weeping ceased and she spoke quietly to Sarah. "I'm sorry I shot at you. I don't know what's come over me. Tom would never forgive me. I'm from an old Southern family, you know, but he loved the Union so."

"Just keep a still tongue in your head when we get to the bridge," Sarah admonished.

They got past the guard at the bridge because it was near two in the morning and he was sleepy. And because Sarah told him the woman she had in tow was Doctor Briscoe's wife, and that her husband was still missing since the battle and they were going to Washington hospitals to locate him.

"Shouldn't let y'all through," the guard said. "But I promised you, Private, that I would. I'm a man of honor. And the doctors worked themselves to the bone in the battle, helping both sides."

When they arrived at Doctor Hammond's hospital tent a clock from a church tower in Washington was eerily striking three in the morning. White tents were ghostly on the hills and campfires flickered. Guards on picket duty stopped Sarah and she had to show the note from Doctor Hammond three times.

She was sick with exhaustion when she delivered Mrs. Briscoe inside. Doctor Hammond had gotten up out of his bed. He looked rumpled and worn, and, in the whispered conversation that followed, thanked her profusely. But tears came into his eyes when Sarah took him aside and told him the story of Mrs. Briscoe.

"She was such a gracious lady, and I knew the two boys," he said. "Thank you, Private Compton, I'll see that she's cared for. You'd best get your rest."

Sarah started for her cot behind the boxes of supplies. As she lay down, she thought she heard Mrs. Briscoe telling Doctor Hammond that the hand wasn't bad. Why, with just a little bandage, she'd be fit to help him in his hospital. Wouldn't he like that? She knew nursing, from helping her husband. Sarah thought she heard Doctor Hammond say yes, that would be fine. But she wasn't sure.

CHAPTER TWELVE

August 15, Camp Winfield Scott, Washington

HEAT AND SULTRINESS SAT ON WASHINGTON like a cover on a pot of boiled squash. But the army continued to drill. Between drillings, the soldiers were taken with lassitude, and lolled around on the green lawns under the trees, talking of home. Sarah tried, as always, not to get too friendly, lest a gesture on her part, or some tale from home, give her away as a woman.

She still hadn't heard anything about Tobias. It was as if he had disappeared into thin air. She ached for Clarice, who'd be mad with worry. Should she write home? No. She'd ask Hammond again if he'd heard anything. Three times in two weeks she asked Fenton if she could again assist Doctor Hammond, but he said no.

"McClellan's orders are more drilling. I can't make an exception for you."

So Sarah was surprised at the end of the second week when she was summoned to Fenton's headquarters. And more than just a little worried, when she saw Doctor Hammond sitting there in a camp chair with his wrist bandaged and a purple bruise on his cheekbone. He did not acknowledge her. He avoided her eyes, as a matter of fact, and Sarah thought it was about Tobias. He'd been killed. But then she remembered that Hammond didn't know Tobias was kin.

She longed to know how Hammond had gotten his wounds.

"You're in trouble, Private Compton," Colonel Fenton said sternly.

Sarah drew herself even more alert and soldierly, and looked past Hammond, trying to conjecture what she'd done, and what it had to do with Hammond. She wished she didn't feel like she used to feel when her father told her she hadn't cleaned out the barn properly, and hoped she'd have the mettle to face whatever had occurred.

"This woman you delivered to Doctor Hammond two weeks ago," Fenton said. "Did you know she was dangerous?"

Oh, Sarah thought. That. And she felt herself letting go of her nervousness just a bit. "She shot at me in front of her house, Sir. Twice. I shot back and wounded her in the hand. I told Doctor Hammond."

"Did you know she was a dyed-in-the-wool Rebel?"

"Not exactly, Sir. I knew she was upset. She said she hated all soldiers and both armies. She said they were crazy. I took it that she was not right in the head because she lost her husband and sons."

"Well, she tried to kill Doctor Hammond," Fenton went on. "She offered to help in the hospital and did well for a while, then yesterday she attacked him with a knife."

Sarah was genuinely aghast. She looked at Doctor Hammond. "I'm sorry, Sir, I didn't know."

Without answering her, Hammond scowled morosely, and waved a hand, dismissing the matter. So, then, what was the problem?

"Why did you bring her back over our lines?" Colonel Fenton asked.

"I had to be back at the Rebel guardhouse on their side of the bridge in two hours, Sir. And she was yelling and taking on in front of her house. She alerted her servants. I knew if they suspected anything was going on they'd get help, I'd be detained and maybe never get back. I had to take her with me. So I put her on the horse behind me."

"And tied her hands in front of you," Colonel Fenton said.

Sarah was more than puzzled now. She was utterly confounded. And when she looked from Fenton to Hammond and perceived that he still would not meet her eyes, she was frightened.

"Yes, Sir. Why?"

"Because," Fenton said, "when she attacked Doctor Hammond and was constrained and threatened with prison, she said she had some important information for us. And that if we promised her safe passage back to her lines, she would disclose it. Do you know what it was, Private Compton?"

"No, Sir."

"She said you are a woman parading as a man. She said when she had her hands tied in front of you, on your uniform blouse she could discern signs that you are a woman. How say you to this charge, Private Compton?"

Sarah felt herself collapsing, falling in on herself. Despair ran through her. She took a quick look at

Hammond, but he appeared betrayed. Yes, she supposed she had betrayed him. And everyone.

"Well, Compton, I'm waiting," Colonel Fenton said. "Do you wish to admit to your sex? Or do you wish to deny it and have Doctor Hammond here examine you?"

Sarah knew a trap when she was in one. There was nothing for it. "I admit it, Sir," she said dismally.

There was a loud noise as Colonel Fenton slammed his hand down on his desk. "Damn," he said. Then he turned to Hammond. "One of my best," he said. "I was going to put him, or her, up for promotion. Isn't that the way of it, Will?"

Doctor Hammond shrugged, still saying nothing. And still not looking at Sarah. What was it now? She'd admitted her deceit. Now he looked as if he was about to betray her.

"This is serious business, Compton. Or whatever your name is. What is it, anyway?"

"Sarah Wheelock, Sir."

"And where did you learn to shoot a gun and march and do all manner of things in the way of a soldier?"

"At home on the farm, Sir. I worked the farm with my sister. I shot game to put food on the family table. Please don't tell my family, Sir, please."

"I'm not worried about your family, Wheelock. I'm worried about you. I'll have to drum you out of the army. There will be punishment. Possibly jail."

"Jail, Sir?" Sarah felt her face go white. Jail for wanting to serve her country?

"I don't know," Fenton said. "There are no rules yet for this kind of infraction. Except taking the oath and lying about it. How old are you, Wheelock?"

"Sixteen," Sarah said miserably.

"Well, you lied under oath about your age, then. Not to mention making a mockery of the army. Serious charges, Wheelock. I'll have to take this up with my superiors. Unless," he hesitated and looked at Doctor Hammond. The look that went between them was heavy with meaning. "Unless you wish to hear the way Doctor Hammond could get you out of this mess, Wheelock. Do you?"

Sarah felt hope. "Yes, Sir. I'll do anything to make amends." Nursing, she thought. They'll be wanting now to make me a female nurse. Word had it that they were flooding Washington, under the supervision of a woman called Dorothea Dix. The doctors did not like them, of course, but she had already worked with Doctor Hammond. He'd seen what she could do. Is that why he was here?

"Doctor?" Colonel Fenton said.

He stood up. He looked down at Sarah, but his look was guarded. He gave no hint of past friendship. "Do you recollect a man who calls himself the Comte de Paris?"

"Yes, Sir. He came to the hospital one day."

"You nurses were putting on an entertainment," Hammond reminded her. "You were playing Topsy. He was much taken with your act."

Sarah only nodded, trying to figure out how this fit in with what they wanted of her. "You want me to entertain for the wounded, sir?" she asked. "Certainly, I can do that. But wouldn't nursing be more useful?"

"Quiet!" Doctor Hammond snapped. "I haven't finished!" He was angry with her.

Meekly, Sarah obeyed.

"I'm not an idiot," Doctor Hammond went on in a softer voice. "Will you just listen? That's why you're in trouble in the first place. Private Compton-Wheelock. Because obviously you don't listen. Obviously you didn't mind your folks at home and ran away. Well, if you want to dislodge yourself from your present misfortune, I'd advise you to start obeying. And start listening."

"I'm listening, Sir," Sarah said. "Only the reason I ran off is because my father wanted to wed me to a man who was twice my age and had the manners of a bear. And I just couldn't do it."

Fenton cleared his throat and looked embarrassed. Doctor Hammond blinked and when he looked at her again there was a sort of tenderness in his eyes, and he gentled his voice but remained firm. "I see. Well, I don't want you to entertain the wounded. The comte is a friend of McClellan's. I am a friend of McClellan's. And McClellan has a friend named Allan Pinkerton. He heads up the Secret Service. And he is in need of operatives."

"Operatives, Sir?" Sarah asked.

"Yes." Hammond began to pace. "Detectives. He employs women as well as men. Your age might go against you. I don't know if he has anyone as young as you. However, this is war. And if I recommend you to McClellan, it would get you off the hook as far as military punishment. You'd get your chance to serve your country, or get away from your family, or whatever it is that you think you're doing hundreds of miles from Michigan. Do you wish me to make this recommendation?"

"I'd rather be a female nurse, Sir. I heard Miss Dix is looking for them."

"You're too young," he said. "I've met Miss Dix. She wants women who are matronly and not pretty. You fail on both requirements."

Sarah found herself blushing. "Well, then, Sir, I'd like to

have a shot at the job with Mr. Pinkerton. I'd like you to recommend me, yes."

Doctor Hammond went to the door of the tent. "Very well then," he said. "Report to my tent this evening. With your permission, Colonel," he nodded at Fenton, "I think she should be out of this camp before word gets around. With your permission, I'll take charge of this matter."

"Gladly, Hammond, and thank you," Colonel Fenton said. Then he looked up at Sarah. "Damn you again for being such a good soldier. And good luck to you," he told her.

CHAPTER THIRTEEN

August 15,
Hospital Number Five, Washington

WHEN SHE GOT TO HOSPITAL NUMBER FIVE THAT night, Doctor Hammond seemed as if he did not quite know how to act toward her. Sarah was still in uniform.

That seemed to bother him. "Have you no other clothes?" he asked.

"No, Sir." She spoke in her normal voice now, not the deeper one she'd affected while playing the part of a soldier, and he noticed that right off.

"You've been feigning a man's voice."

"Yes, Sir."

"That must have been a strain."

"Yes, Sir. Times it was."

He nodded and sighed. "Tomorrow we meet with Pinkerton. Tonight you sleep in the room where I keep the medicines. Auntie Narcissa is making up a cot for you in there now. Have you eaten? There's a pot of stew on the fire."

She ate and went to bed in a small room the size of a closet. Next morning there was a complete outfit of women's clothing laid over a chair, everything from underthings and stockings to a skirt, blouse, and plain straw hat. There was a basin of water, small bar of scented soap, and a container of sweet-smelling powder, as well as a comb and brush.

Sarah was startled at the thoughtfulness of whoever had done this. And touched. The clothes were freshly laundered and ironed. The skirt was dark blue sprigged with tiny pink flowers. The shirtwaist she recognized as a Garibaldi blouse, the kind with no collar but a little puffing at the top of the full sleeves. She hadn't had on girls' clothing in months now. She supposed she was to put the things on. So she washed herself and got dressed, then peeked out into the main part of the hospital.

The male nurses were already going about their morning chores. The men were up and several nodded and smiled at her as they were having their breakfasts. Some of the nurses did, too. To them the sight of a woman in the hospital was a welcome sight.

She helped herself to a cup of coffee. Auntie Narcissa was cooking on the stove and gave her a broad smile. "Well, those clothes fit jus' fine."

"Did you get them for me?" Sarah asked.

The woman nodded her turbaned head in the direction of Doctor Hammond, who was changing a man's bandage at the other end of the tent. "Yes, but he tol' me jus' what to get, right down to the comb and brush." She chuckled. "Here, have some breakfast. Gonna be a long, hot day."

She sat and ate in a corner of the hospital and before she was finished Doctor Hammond came over with some nurses to give them their orders for the day and go over some instructions.

Again, none of the men recognized her. And when they left to go about their duties, Doctor Hammond glanced at her, sat down at his table, and said without looking up, "Well, you've passed the first test, anyway."

"Sir?"

Still, he did not look up but was intent on his writing. "The men didn't recognize you. That should count for something in the spy business. But then, you're an expert at fooling people, aren't you?"

There was a hard edge to his voice and it made Sarah want to cry. "Sir, I'd hoped you wouldn't stay angry with me for what I've done."

"I'm not angry. Disappointed, perhaps, but not angry. Are you finished with breakfast?"

"Yes, Sir."

"Then let's get on our way to meet Pinkerton."

Sarah did not know what to expect when they drove through the streets of Washington in Doctor Hammond's trap, pulled by a horse he kept in a nearby stable, but she thought they would go to Mr. Pinkerton's office, wherever that was.

He spoke little on the way, but as a group of ducks scattered in front of them, he did say one thing. "You don't have to do this, Sarah. I have the authority to send you to Dorothea Dix. I don't want you further endangered."

"I'll be able to handle myself, sir," she said.

"Make sure of it. If you decide not to go with Pinkerton, come back and see me."

Sarah promised she would. Then they pulled up in front of Thompson's Drugstore. Doctor Hammond led her to a glass-topped table. Just as they'd sat down and ordered some of the confection, a man in a plaid coat, bowler hat, and full beard sat down with them and ordered some vanilla ice cream.

"This is Mr. Pinkerton," Doctor Hammond said. "He is known here in Washington as Major Allan. Major, this is Sarah Wheelock."

Immediately, Sarah recognized the man who'd stopped her and Nubbin on the street earlier on the same day she'd gone to Dr. Briscoe's house.

"I have heard of your exploits," Pinkerton said. "You must have excellent acting abilities, my dear. To have lasted nearly three months in the army without discovery is to your credit. And I've been told you are an expert at mimicry. That little skit you put on for the soldiers the day the Comte de Paris saw you. You played Topsy, did you not?"

"Yes, Sir."

"It is the best here," he said, referring to the vanilla ice cream. And when it came he spooned it delicately into his mouth while he spoke. "I understand you left home to get away from a domineering father. Why didn't you just run away? Why didn't you try to get into the new nursing corps? Why the army?"

"I wanted to serve my country," Sarah said simply.

"In my service you will serve your country better than on the field," Pinkerton said. "I have several female operatives. If you agree to come aboard you will go in training with the head of my female detectives, Kate Warne. She is a resourceful and dependable woman. She has never let me down. And, after about a week with Kate, if she approves you and you agree, I have a special assignment for you. Right here in Washington."

Sarah nodded. She liked Major Allan. He was modest and gentle and he spoke with reverence of his female detectives. She agreed to work a week with Kate Warne.

"Good." Major Allan smiled. "If you will stay here when Doctor Hammond and I leave, and order another portion of ice cream, she will be along directly and take you in hand." He stood up. "I understand Doctor Hammond has taken on the role of your protector. My dear, you could have none better. But once in my employ you may not contact him. If he wishes to keep track of you, well, that's his business. Is that to your liking?"

Never in all her life had Sarah had anyone ask what was to her liking.

She said yes.

Doctor Hammond and Major Allan stood. Major Allan paid the bill, nodded at her, and left. Doctor Hammond stood there in his rumpled linen jacket, his cravat a little lopsided, his straw hat in his hand. "Well, Sarah," he said. "So we come to a parting of the ways."

A sense of loss tore at her insides as she looked up at this dear man who had been so good to her and who felt so betrayed by her deception. "I'll make you proud," she said.

"Keep safe. That will make me happy. Godspeed." He held out his hand.

Sarah had never shaken hands with a man before. She'd seen women having their hands kissed by men and always thought it a bit silly. Now she stood up and reached her hand across the table. Doctor Hammond's hand was firm and strong. And Sarah felt honored by the gesture, more honored than any pretentious hand-kissing could make her feel. Then Doctor Hammond turned on his heel and left.

Sarah ordered more vanilla ice cream and waited.

One of the best things about working at the Seventh Street Ferry House, Sarah decided, was that the cooling air off the river fanned your face. One of the worst things was the smells. Washington was full of smells in the summer, from open sewers, pigs roaming the streets, and cattle and horses of the army. But here, in southwest Washington, which was divided from the rest of the city by the old canal, you got the full complement of river air at the confluence of the Potomac and the Eastern Branch.

It was called Greenleaf's Point. Here at the foot of Sixth and Seventh Streets, Sarah could see the red brick spires of the Smithsonian Institution, as well as the steamboats and sailing ships that brought people to and from the railroads at Alexandria or Aquia Creek.

Some of the boats made the voyage to the Chesapeake Bay and the ocean beyond. People of all kinds came and went.

And the normal smells here, including that of Swampoodle, the poor Irish colony in the nearby marshy tract, were carried on the river breezes. At Kate's instruction, Sarah carried a lavender-soaked handkerchief with her to put over her nose when it got especially bad.

Their job was to search women who were getting off and going on the ferries. They searched for contraband inside their dresses at their bosoms, in extra-large bustles behind their dresses, even in their hair. Sometimes that contraband was messages, sometimes it was opium or quinine to be smuggled south.

"Women make the best spies," Kate told her. "They have so many places on their person to hide things."

Kate was a widow. She'd been with Major Allan since 1856, when she walked into his Chicago office one morning and told him she wanted to be a detective. At that time she was twenty-three. Now, five years later, she was slender, brown-haired, and had a pleasant face that was attractive, Sarah decided, more for its lively intelligence than its looks.

"You should have seen Major Allan when I walked in that day," she told Sarah. "He was so amazed at the idea of a female detective that he said he had to think about it. Then he said he stayed up half the night conjecturing. And wondering why the notion hadn't come to him first."

Kate treated Sarah like a sister. She brought her to her rooms on H Street, gave her an allowance for clothing, and helped her assemble a wardrobe that was in keeping with her needs. Plain but not dowdy. Sarah even had one hoop, in case she had to appear at a proper function.

Sarah had never had a girl for a friend. At home, she and Betsy had always been too busy getting the farmwork done, too worn down at night to talk or confide in each other before going to sleep. Kate knew how to maneuver the tricky balancing act of being both boss and friend. She taught Sarah how to assess people; how to tell, by their body movements, if they were lying. She even taught her some quick movements of self-defense. And she knew her way around Washington.

This new experience of another woman's innocent

companionship was like a gift to Sarah, like a wine she had never tasted. She savored it, and sometimes, like wine, it made her giddy with happiness.

Sometimes other detectives came to Kate's rooms on H Street to compare notes, to exchange information, or just to talk.

Sarah had already met Hattie Lawton, another female operative, as well as Seth Pain, John Babcock, who'd been a crack shot with the Sturgis Rifle Corps in Chicago, and John Scully, who'd been born in England.

Some agents were now behind enemy lines. One, Timothy Webster, had been sent in June to Baltimore, "to lay pipe with the disloyalists." Hattie Lawton had posed as his wife, and Webster was responsible, Sarah learned, for giving Pinkerton the names of many spies. He'd given the name of Rose Greenhow, the woman on Sixteenth Street who'd given Sarah and Nubbin the bottle of wine that morning for the hospital. Greenhow was soon to be placed under arrest.

By Thursday of the first week, Sarah had already caught a woman who was leaving on the ferry to bring a supply of morphine across Southern lines and another who had two bottles of good Southern whiskey, laced with a poisonous substance, in her bodice. She was on her way to visit some Northern soldiers who were hospitalized.

"These Southern Rebel women are the most demented about their cause," Kate said.

Sarah told her about Doctor Briscoe's wife and how the woman had tried to shoot her, and then kill Doctor Hammond.

On Friday Sarah spied a suspicious-looking woman who was about to board the ferry. She was dressed as a man, but she walked like a woman, something Sarah herself had been careful not to do in her tenure as a soldier. For another, she had not bothered to bind up her bosom. Sarah herself accosted her. "Can you spare us a minute, Ma'am?"

The woman immediately tried to run, but Sarah had her hand firmly on her arm. There was a brief struggle, and she almost did get away but for Kate, who came to help, and in a minute the two of them had her off to the side. Kate led her to the small room where they confronted their suspects, examined her trunk and found morphine, opium, quinine, a revolver, a pair of military spurs, and an iron projectile. She first gave her name as John Barton, then admitted she was a Mrs. McCarty from Philadelphia.

The iron projectile, she said, was her husband's invention. It could take a person's head off at two hundred yards, and she was on her way to Richmond to sell it to the Confederates.

"You're good," Kate told her at day's end. "I would have missed that one dressed as a man. I'm going to tell Major Allan that as far as I'm concerned, you're approved, and should be started on your next assignment."

August 24, Kate Warne's House on H Street

"I'm assigning you to Fort Greenhow, Sarah," Major Allan said.

They were seated under the oil lamp that hung over the table in Kate Warne's kitchen, having coffee and cake Kate had made that afternoon on her day off.

"Fort Greenhow?" Sarah asked. Was there a fort named after the Washington socialite he'd just had placed under arrest? Kate had told her about Rose Greenhow's past, how she'd been a society belle in President James Buchanan's administration. How she had the admiration of statesmen, diplomats, generals, and legislators. And in her Sixteenth Street house, she'd entertained them all.

She was a widow, Kate had said. She lived with her eight-year-old daughter. Two other daughters were out west. One had just died.

"My operatives who've been watching her house for

weeks named it Fort Greenhow," Major Allen explained. "My male detectives keep her under constant watch, but she has complained about them. She is a she-devil. I fear she is still gathering military information and sending it on to Richmond. She must be watched every minute. But I want you to go as a lady-in-waiting, if you will. A maid. Earn her confidence, so you can move about freely among her things. So she trusts you. Do you think you can do that?"

Sarah didn't answer for a moment, not out of self-doubt but because she was so enamored of the idea. She remembered the brick mansion that Nubbin had pointed out to her, and how the woman had sent the sparkling wine, and how Doctor Hammond had been so enraged that Sarah had accepted it. Had he known about Mrs. Greenhow then?

Major Allen leaned forward at the table. "Sarah, this woman is responsible for the deaths of thousands of Union soldiers at Manassas. It was because of her correspondence with leaders in Richmond, her information about the number of troops we had, and the exact time of their movements that we lost the battle."

"I'll do it, Sir," Sarah said.

CHAPTER FOURTEEN

August 27, Fort Greenhow, Washington

THE LITTLE GIRL WAS IN THE LARGE, GNARLED APPLE tree behind the house. Sarah heard her before she saw her. "My mother's been arrested," she was screaming from halfway up the tree. "My mother's been arrested."

In the backyard of the house, which was surrounded on three sides by a tall fence, Sarah saw men trying to get the little girl down. She recognized two of them as belonging to the Sturgis Rifles, who were always guarding the place. And the other as Pryce Lewis, one of Pinkerton's men. He was English, very tall and amiable, wore side whiskers, and had a hearty sense of humor.

The little girl was done up in a crisp frock, under which frothed many ruffled petticoats, and her hair was pulled back in a cascade of curls. That must be Little Rose, Sarah decided. She was pelting the three men with old apples and using language such as Sarah had heard out of the mouths of men from the 2nd Michigan.

The men could not get up the tree. And the little girl's screams would soon attract attention. Sarah put down her portmanteau and ran into the backyard. "I'll get her down," she offered. "I'm Mrs. Greenhow's maid, Sarah Dawson, come to report for work today. Let me try, please."

Pryce Lewis winked at her. Though he knew her, he was not allowed to acknowledge it. He introduced her to the others, who were from Pinkerton's bodyguard unit. "This is Sergeant Mark Stevens of the Sturgis Rifles. And Lieutenant Sheldon. And that's the Rebel spy-in-training up there," he said.

Sarah had been warned of Sheldon by Kate Warne. He was, she noted now, as handsome and debonair as described. She saw immediately the expensive broadcloth of his uniform, that his shirt was made of Irish linen, and the twinkle in his eye had not been exaggerated. "Cock of the rock," Kate had told her. "A popinjay. All the women swoon over him. Major Allen is worried he'll fall under Mrs. Greenhow's spell. You'll have to keep an eye out for that and let us know if it happens."

"Can you climb the tree?" Pryce asked.

"I've been climbing trees on my father's farm since I was three," Sarah told him. And saw the distaste on Sheldon's face. She ran to her portmanteau to get out the small china doll she'd brought along for Rose. When she'd been briefed about her duties, she knew she'd have to win over the child. With the doll in hand she placed one foot firmly on the gnarled branch and proceeded her ascent.

"Come on down, Rose, honey," she begged.

"Don't you call me honey, you dried-up old maid."

It rankled Sarah that a child should be allowed to use such language. If ever she and Betsy had spoken so they would have felt the back of their father's hand. Then she stopped such thoughts. Isaac had been no measure of fatherhood, and this child had no father. And she and her mother were now prisoners. She started climbing. "I am a maid. You've got that part right. I'm your mama's new maid, come to help her and serve her. I can serve you, too. You'll be a real little lady. Won't you like that?"

"I deserve that," the child said. "I'm quality."

"Of course, you are. I could see that right off. And here,

I've brought you a new little play-pretty. Look." Sarah held out the doll and saw the round little face flush with greed.

"Give it to me here and now," the child demanded.

"Oh, but you must come down and act like a little lady of quality. They don't receive people in trees."

"All right, I'll come down, but you're only a maid. And you aren't received anywhere. Remember your place."

"I shall," Sarah said, "I promise." Then she reached out to take the child's hand, balanced herself on the tree branch, and managed to turn and hand her over to Lewis's outstretched arms.

"Jolly good," Lewis said as he set her on the ground.

Then, to Sarah's surprise, she saw Little Rose hold out her hand and Lieutenant Sheldon bow and kiss it.

"Come," Little Rose directed, snapping her fingers at Sarah, "and I shall take you to my mama."

Sarah had been well coached by Kate Warne before she even approached the elegant two-story pink-brick house on Sixteenth Street.

Three things were all she had to really know about Rose Greenhow. She had supplied the Southern general Pierre Beauregard with the Union plans for Bull Run. She ran a network of at least fifty spies. And somehow, she was still transmitting secrets to the Confederate capital. Pinkerton's spies in Richmond had reported to him that messages were still getting through.

Part of Sarah's job was to find out how.

Rose was expecting her. She'd been told that an old friend from the Buchanan administration, hearing of her distress, had supplied her with a personal maid. Rose's house had been stripped of most of its furniture and she was left with the simplest of appointments so she couldn't hide things. Although many secret papers had already been discovered, there was still a diary to be found.

That was to be part of Sarah's job, too.

"Pinkerton knows of the diary," Kate had said. "You cannot be apprised of how. Just look for it. And when you find it, get it directly out of the house to our intermediary."

That was another thing Sarah must keep in mind. The minute she went through the wrought-iron front gate of the pale pink-brick house with the white shutters, for all intents and purposes she, too, would be a prisoner of sorts.

No one inside was to know she worked for Pinkerton. If they were Pinkerton people they would treat her like a maid.

She was to be in contact with no one on the outside. Not even on her day off, which was Saturday. Not even Doctor Hammond.

Her only outside contact would be the woman at Drayton's Confectioners at the corner, where Rose frequently sent her guards for treats for her child. Iris, her name was. Sarah was always to ask for Iris, and deal with no one else.

"Once you go into Mrs. Greenhow's house, you're on your own," Kate had told her. "You are to use your own instincts, your own judgment. And trust no one."

"Mother, your maid is here." Little Rose ran into the library that adjoined Rose's bedroom, and into her mother's arms.

"Ah, perhaps I shall now be able to live up to my station somewhat." The woman called Rose Greenhow and known as "The Wild Rose," sat in a chair at a desk, writing. Sarah had heard so much about her she was almost afraid to meet her. But she was smaller than Sarah expected. She was wearing black. And her hair, which might have once been luxuriant, was streaked with gray. In her forties, they'd told Sarah.

Like my mother, Sarah had thought. But this woman, though showing signs of age, was not worn like Sarah remembered her mother to be. Her hands were not rough. And her eyes sparkled. Sarah had never seen her mother's eyes sparkle.

"Your name, dear," Rose Greenhow asked.

"Sarah Dawson, Ma'am," Sarah gave a little curtsy and saw Rose's eyes light up.

"And where do you hail from?"

"Missouri, Ma'am. I came when the war started, as a maid for the Walworths. My mother was distant kin to his wife."

The name, and everything Sarah told Rose, had been carefully rehearsed. Her previous employer should be somebody Rose Greenhow had heard of, but never personally known.

"Ah, I heard of their misfortune. He was in the War Department, wasn't he?"

"Yes, Ma'am, but because his wife had connections to the South his house was searched and a Confederate lieutenant's uniform was found in his trunk. They were sent home to Virginia."

"It's such a shame." Rose sighed heavily. "All my friends have been scattered. Washington is ruined." Sarah thought there was somewhat of a petulant whine in her voice, and could see where Little Rose got her manners from.

"No more parties like there used to be," the woman went on. "The Lincolns don't know how to entertain. They are barbarians. There is a quartermaster's depot on the White House grounds. Imagine! Corcoran's Art Gallery is a clothing depot. Senator Gwin's house is the headquarters of the military governor and the Old Capitol a Rebel prison. General Scott's home is a boardinghouse and thousands of drunken demoralized soldiers are in the streets, crowding women into the gutters, and shouting obscenities. Oh, dear, I could use some tea."

"I'll make some, Ma'am," Sarah said. And she turned to leave the room, then stopped, awkwardly. "There is just one thing, Ma'am."

Rose Greenhow, the "romantic rebel of Sixteenth Street" as she was called, met Sarah's eyes, then took her measure. Sarah felt naked and exposed. "Yes?"

"The only way I was permitted to come and serve you, I am given to understand, is if I sleep in your room. Mr. Pinkerton demanded it."

"I know. Pinkerton! The devil's henchman. The German-Jew detective."

"I heard he was a Scot, Ma'am."

"He invaded my Gertrude's room when he searched my house. Did you see the painting of the lovely girl downstairs?"

Sarah allowed that she had.

"That's my Gertrude. She died when that ape, Lincoln, was inaugurated. Pinkerton touched her things! I haven't touched her things since she died! He swept aside all her toilet articles, her books, then took them. In my mind he is a German Jew!"

"Yes, Ma'am, I'm sorry. Is there anything you'd like with the tea?"

"They allow us so little here. Ask that nice Lieutenant Sheldon to go to the confectioner's and get some iced cakes. We'll have a tea party, won't we, Rose?" She looked at the little girl who was sitting on the floor. She appeared to be playing with her new doll. But Sarah had the feeling she was listening to every word being said.

"If you wish, Mama."

Sara curtsied again and went down to find the kitchen.

CHAPTER FIFTEEN

August 27, Later That Night, Fort Greenhow, Washington

THE FIRST THING SARAH FELT SHE SHOULD DO WAS get to know the lay of the house. You could tell a lot about people from their house, she had learned. Look at Ma's two-story structure, stark, weatherbeaten, with a front porch held up by rickety posts, as if it might collapse at any moment. And windows that stared at you like eyes without hope.

Look at Aunt Annie's cottage in Flint, with the store

downstairs, the porch with fat posts, the door painted a bright yellow, and the upstairs rooms cheerful and filled with books and flowers and colorful chintz curtains and settees.

Besides, she might have to make a quick exit out of Rose's house sometime. And she'd been instructed to go to the windows in the front parlor and raise and lower the shade three times if she was in trouble. Outside, the Sturgis Rifles would know what to do.

She studied the kitchen first. Though there were no signs that it had been recently used — no food in the larder, no leftovers in the box that should have been filled with ice — there were huge platters and linen tablecloths stored in cupboards and the stove was one such as she'd never seen before. Cast iron, it was a monstrosity, with four fireboxes on top. In the section below a mildly warm fire was burning.

"You'll never be able to figure it out. Not one of us has." Sarah turned to see Lieutenant Sheldon standing in the doorway to the hall. "But don't worry, you won't have to cook on it. The food is sent in each day."

"I just want to make her some tea," Sarah said.

He showed her how to set the water on the right part of the range, how to put wood in the firebox to build up the blaze without burning her fingers.

"You look at home in a kitchen," she said. "Not like my brother, Ben."

He laughed. "When I was younger I spent a lot of time in the kitchen with Auntie Moon. We called her that because she had a round moon face. She gave me goodies and listened to my woes."

"Where is home?" Sarah asked. It was always good to know everything you could about your colleagues, Kate Warne had told her. Sarah had learned a lot from Kate. She hadn't even known the meaning of the word "colleagues" before. It sounded important.

"Hagerstown, Maryland."

So his family could go either way. North or South. "Was Auntie Moon a slave?" she asked delicately, "or a paid servant?"

"I know Maryland is pretty well split down the middle. But my family is loyal to the Union, if that's what you're asking. How about yours? Missouri has more troubles than Maryland."

"The same. But at home we still do the old-type hearth cooking."

There was an awkward silence, in which Sarah perceived somehow that he was lying to her about everything. The same as she was to him. This business of being a spy was a contrary affair, she determined. She was accustomed to honesty in her dealings with people. Now she had to watch every word she said, lest she be tricked. And the funny part about it was that they were both likely on the same side.

"Look," Sheldon said, "I'm going to the confectioner's. Would you like some cake? I have been allotted a certain amount of money every day to run errands for her."

"Don't you feel put upon?" Sarah asked. "After all, you're a member of McClellan's personal bodyguard. Running errands for a spy!"

"She's only doing what she thinks best for her country. She's a precious nice lady when you get to know her."

Sarah felt her hackles rise. "Oh? Have you gotten to know her, then?"

"Somewhat. I know she seems onerous at first. And contrary. But she's still in mourning for Gertrude. We must give her some latitude. How would you like it if your mother was a prisoner?"

But she is, Sarah thought. In her own way. No, she could not conjure up sympathy for Rose Greenhow, if only because she'd had the benefit of all life's fripperies, when her own mama was lucky to have one new calico dress a year and never saw people except once a week at church.

"She caused the deaths of thousands at Bull Run," she reminded him.

"She's done no more than our spies have done and are doing."

Sarah knew she shouldn't take sides, that as Sarah Dawson she should have Southern leanings, if any. And he could be testing her, to see who she really was. She had the feeling that Sheldon was not as innocent as he contrived to appear. "I'll try to understand her," she said. "And I would like a cake, yes."

"Oh, I should tell you," he said as he turned to go. "Lily Mackall is coming this evening. She is a fast friend of Rose's. Her husband is assistant adjunct general of the Confederate forces. She will be allowed to come and go as she pleases."

Sarah blinked in surprise. "Why?"

"In hopes that she will lead us to others. Or drop information. She's harmless." He grinned, and something inside Sarah rose, then fell. He did have beautiful white teeth. And there was something of the little mischievous boy in the grin. He was handsome. And he knew it. She found herself blushing, as if the grin were an audacious move on his part, as if he knew its magic and used it like his rifle, to disarm someone.

"Yes," he went on, "the authorities are allowing certain people in to freely associate with Rose. To be watched. And learned from. Although," he looked around with exaggerated interest, "I can't say who around here is supposed to be learning her secrets. Can you?"

In that moment Sarah knew that Lieutenant Sheldon, cock of the rock, popinjay in residence, knew she was that person. "No, I can't," she said.

"And of course you know about Lizzy Fitzgerald, Little Rose's nurse. This is her afternoon off. She'll be back soon, also."

"Nurse," she found herself saying dumbly. Was the child sickly, then?

"Yes, you don't think that girl stays in those starched petticoats and shiny curls because of her mother's efforts, do you? All proper Southern children have nurses."

Sarah thought of herself at eight, in homespun muslin, already slopping Pa's hogs, picking beans, and weeding corn. "Sorry, I wasn't thinking," she said. She must think, however. She must stop being the country bumpkin. She must think about the elegance and advantages in Rose's life.

"Don't worry about answering the door," he said as he went out. "The Sturgis Rifles are responsible for letting everyone in and out. That's not your job. And Rose is allowed other visitors. Important people come and go. They're all being watched, don't worry."

Some prisoner, Sarah thought. But she only nodded

and could not help admiring him, the little half bow he gave, the way he turned on his heel in military fashion, the confident set of his shoulders. I have lived in a half-world all my life, she told herself. I am wanting. There is much for me to learn. And I must set myself to the task.

After Sheldon went out the front door, she walked quietly through the house. It was stripped of most of its furnishings, yes, but no one could take the charm away from the tall windows from which silken draperies hung, the chandeliers in the dining room and parlor. There were really two parlors, divided by crimson portieres that looked to be of the most expensive silk. In one parlor were walls of books with dark covers and gold writing. Sarah had never seen so many books. And there was an intricate iron grate in front of the fireplace and a rosewood pianoforte. On the wall were portraits in gold frames. George Washington and Benjamin Franklin, of course, but who were the others?

It riled her that she did not know. She must not be ignorant. Rose would expect her to know.

"That's President Buchanan," a small voice piped in back of Sarah. "Mama was very close to him. She wore diamonds in her hair on his inauguration day. When he fell ill while staying at the National Hotel just before he was sworn in, they said that it was because infected rats fell into the hotel's water tanks. Mama never believed it. She thinks he was poisoned."

For a moment Sarah was too startled to say anything.

"For a long time afterward, Buchanan had to drink tumblers of whiskey every day to rid himself of the poison. Only my mama knew that. Have you ever seen Robert Lincoln?"

"No, I haven't."

"They say he is most handsome. How do you suppose an ape like Lincoln gets to have a handsome son?"

"Well, his wife is quite nice-looking."

"Mama says she is too short, her complexion is terrible, and she is pretentious."

"We can't help what God made us," Sarah said.

"I suppose not." Rose twirled around a bit, showing the flounces under her dress. "Did you know I have a brother-in-law who is a quartermaster in the Union army? And a cousin in the 1st Rhode Island Volunteers? And another cousin who was married to Stephen Douglas, who died just last June?"

"No, I didn't." Sarah started to fix the pillows on the only settee in the parlor.

"There's lots you don't know," the child said. "You'd better learn. My mama doesn't countenance ignorance. And you needn't look for my mama's diary, either."

Startled, Sarah straightened herself up and went rigid. "I wasn't. What diary?"

"Everybody who comes here looks for it." The little girl giggled. "They ask me. As if I'll tell. Do you know what I want most in the world right now?"

Sarah was afraid to ask, so she just shook her head, no.

"I want to go to a party. I had a lot of friends here in Washington, and I went to parties all the time before Mama got herself arrested. I still get invitations. But Mama said no, that other children will ask me questions about her and embarrass me and make me feel bad. But they are my friends and I long to see them. If I give you a riddle as to where the diary is, would you ask Mama to let me go to my friend Adele's party next week?"

Sarah could not believe her good fortune. She would not allow herself to believe it. If only she could find the diary! She'd manage something no other operative had been able to do! "Of course, I'll ask her," she said. "But why would I want your mama's diary?"

"Because everybody does. And, anyway, it's a game. But you'll never figure out the riddle."

"So tell it to me then."

"No. Not now. When I'm ready. The water is boiling for tea."

CHAPTER SIXTEEN

August 28, Fort Greenhow, Washington

THE NEXT DAY SARAH HAD A NOTE FROM LITTLE Rose. She had put it in the pocket of the apron Sarah wore. Somehow she had slipped into the room Sarah was obliged to sleep in with her mother, which was locked from the outside at night while a Sturgis Rifle man stood guard. On some pretense Little Rose had gotten past the guard. Finding the note that morning, Sarah began to realize that this child was someone to be reckoned with.

She took the note to the dressing room where she

would complete her toilet. Before she had a chance to read it, Mrs. Greenhow rang the little silver bell she'd taken to using to summon her. Sarah sighed. The sound of the bell was already tearing at her nerves and she hadn't been here twenty-four hours yet.

"I wish my breakfast, when it comes, to be served here" — Rose gestured to a small table in the corner of the room — "on the embroidered cloth you will find in the kitchen cupboard. I wish you to use my silver coffee urn this morning. I'll breakfast with Lily Mackall. And I want the cream-colored china with the blue flowers."

Sarah nodded and started downstairs, pulling the note from her pocket and reading as she went. It said: "Here is my riddle. Figure it out if you can.

"Salome had her seven veils, myself I have none, but if you see me stare at you, you'll know my tears make one."

Sarah read it three or four times, befuddled. Her mouth was dry and her head hurt. It had been hot in the upstairs bedroom and the cot on which she slept was none too comfortable. She needed a cup of tea and went into the kitchen to get it.

"Hello! You're the maid, aren't you?"

The woman in the kitchen wore a silk wrapper. She was tall and thin and the wrapper, which had some kind of Oriental design, was open enough at the bottom so as to reveal a long, thin leg. Her hair was braided up on top of her head with just enough tendrils falling about her face to soften it. She wore an expression of placid self-satisfaction.

"Well, aren't you? I'd heard there was a maid here! God, this is a dismal place now. Nothing like it was when Rose was in the midst of society and entertaining all the time. The food! Wild turkey, pigeon, terrapin, and black bass from the Potomac. You can't imagine! Well," and she looked around haughtily, "they've made a prison out of this elegant house, to be sure. Only Northerners can do that."

Sarah stood transfixed. The woman had the bearing of a queen, and she was only a year or two older than Sarah. How did young women get to be this way? she wondered. Who gave them the right to this commanding, self-assured demeanor? Then, in a moment, she answered her own question. The Southern dialect. Of course! Women in the South, in the slave states, were accustomed to ordering people about, accustomed to being revered.

"I'm Sarah Dawson," she said.

"I'm Lily Mackall, Rose's friend. And there is one thing you and all here should know. Rose Greenhow is a very dear friend to me. I would do anything for her. I will pound on the front door of the White House if I have to and get that ape to free her. The injustice of it, keeping her and her child here like this when she just lost a daughter and has no husband! You may bring my tea into the parlor. When does that strutting peacock from the Sturgis Rifles come in with breakfast?"

Sarah assumed she meant Sheldon. "I don't know. This is my first morning here."

"This is a fine woman," she said again of Rose. "Did you know that her father was killed by his Negro body servant when she was just a child?"

"No."

"Any wonder she takes up the cause of the Confederacy? She has no husband, you know, no defender. He took a fall in California and died, right after Little Rose was born."

"I'm sorry to hear that," Sarah returned, all the while thinking, *Rose needs no defender. Something tells me we need to be defended from her.*

Lily Mackall waved a hand, as if someone as lowborn as Sarah could not possibly comprehend the true tragedy or majesty of the situation, and strode out of the room. All the while Sarah was searching her mind for some reference to the name. Lily Mackall. Kate hadn't told Sarah about her. Was Lily supposed to be here? Did Pinkerton know? Sarah doubted that he missed anything that was going on inside the house. Likely his guards outside knew that Sarah was making tea this very minute.

Am I supposed to be a maid for Lily Mackall, too? she wondered. She knew the answer to that. Yes, if it got the job done. She set herself to the task of making tea, going over and over in her mind the riddle Little Rose had written.

From upstairs could be heard the child's voice as her nurse readied her for the day. What was to be the nature of things between her and Little Rose? Had the child told her mother of the riddle? Or was it a secret that Little Rose was using to get a favor in return?

My first day here, Sarah thought, and already I have a headache from the job. I'd rather be back at Camp Winfield Scott, drilling.

Sarah fetched a cup of tea into the parlor for Lily, who sat on the single settee reading a copy of *Harpers New Monthly Magazine*. Then she assembled what Rose required, the silver coffee urn, the dishes for breakfast, and the embroidered cloth, and brought them all upstairs and set the small table.

Just in time, too. Because Lieutenant Sheldon and one of the men from the Sturgis Rifles came up with the breakfast sent over every morning by the confectioner's.

"I've managed to secure some excellent French pastry

for the occasion." Sheldon set the paper package down and bowed to Lily Mackall, who had just come into the room. But his eyes, Sarah noted, were on Rose.

"Dear boy, what would I do without you?" Rose asked.

Sarah saw Sheldon blush, and thought, "Why he's smitten with her! And she so much older than him!" The thought repelled her for some reason and she felt anger at Rose.

She lingered long enough to see that the coffee, sent in a tin container, was transferred into the silver urn, that she herself poured it, that everything was as perfect as could be. She wondered about the people at the corner confectioner's, the very place where her contact was. Then she began to wonder about the peculiarity of the whole situation. No one, she decided, was who they seemed to be in this house. Everyone was acting. And you couldn't be certain of anything or anybody.

Lily and Rose complained about the food.

"Mush," Rose called it.

"Tavern fare," Lily said.

"French pastry?" Rose asked. "That boy is sadly uneducated. But what do you expect from Northerners?"

Sarah felt embarrassed for Sheldon. Rose did not return his feelings. She was using him. She felt anger at the woman, who was dallying with the handsome young man.

Rose and Lily talked about breakfasts past then, of fish and potatoes and lobster in sauce and eggs and the very best of Southern ham. And coffee with gallons of cream and cinnamon cake and biscuits light as a cloud.

Then they spoke of Little Rose. "She shows her breeding to great advantage," Lily was saying. And Rose preened. And Sarah thought, Does everyone pander to her? Right about then she left the room and went downstairs.

What did Salome's seven veils have to do with it? Was the diary hidden behind something that looked like a veil? A curtain, perhaps. And what was meant by "but if you see me stare at you"? And how could tears make a veil? Sarah pondered until her head hurt so badly she had to finally put the note aside and eat some breakfast herself. It was growing hot already. Late August in Washington was living up to its reputation. What was it Doctor Hammond had said? "So hot it was like the inside of the devil's lying throat."

When she went back upstairs after eating alone in the kitchen, Sarah passed Lily's room and saw her lying on the bed, the window open, in her drawers and chemise. To Sarah's startled stare she responded, "If the guards are embarrassed, they needn't look. Why should I swelter because of them?"

Rose was already fanning herself, but she had other things on her mind. As Sarah collected the breakfast dishes, which she supposed she would be obliged to wash, Rose recounted her requests.

"I wish some writing materials today. You must get word to that odious man Pinkerton that I am to be permitted the use of paper and pen and ink. How else can I continue my daughter's lessons? And my tapestry. It becalms me. I must be able to do my needlework."

"I am not in touch with Mr. Pinkerton, Ma'am," Sarah said.

"I'll get them for you." Lily appeared in the hall, still in her long ruffled drawers and chemise. "I do have some influence."

Sarah did not linger. As she made her way precariously down the stairs with the tray of dirty dishes, she heard them talking about the dinners Rose had attended at the White House when Pierce was president, how the bouquets on the table had been so large, and how the gold spoons that were President Monroe's legacy had glowed in the candlelight.

Sarah was to have an hour off each afternoon, and Rose requested that she take it from one until two, the hottest part of the day. This was her time to nap. Sarah was to open the windows to let in the air on the cool side of the room and pull down all the green paper shades with the flowers painted on the edges. She had to admit it did give the room a cooling effect.

Little Rose was made to take a nap, too. That first day Sarah changed into a lighter muslin dress and betook herself to the backyard under the old apple tree, which gave good shade. In her hands were a glass of lemonade and two sugar cookies. In her pocket was Little Rose's riddle.

She sat down on the grass. From the other side of the tall fence came street sounds, the clopping of horses pulling carriages, snatches of conversation as people went by, and in the distance the tolling of a church bell. But the other side of the fence was another world, where people went about freely, where they did not pretend to be other than who they were. Where one did not have to watch one's every utterance, lest it be taken as having a double meaning.

She closed her eyes and leaned her head against the sturdy tree trunk, the paper with the riddle on it in her hand.

"I see Little Rose has snagged you now to do her dirty work."

Her eyes flew open. Lieutenant Sheldon stood there. Sarah's first thought was, how does he stay so crisp and fresh in this heat? She thought then that part of it was that he was clean-shaven. It was so nice to see a man without a bushy beard on his face. And she decided that this lack of mustache and beard, which exposed his expression, was what drew her to him. There was something going on between his eyes and his smile. They cooperated, each complementing and supporting the other. Sarah decided that he was upright and good, and this parrying of words that so far had gone on between them was a defense both were using to hold the other at bay. Because they both had secrets.

His cap was tucked under one arm. He leaned the butt of his rifle on the ground. "She gave you the riddle, didn't she? In return for a favor. What does she want this time? Some stick candy? Ice cream? Or be allowed to sneak out the gate?"

"What riddle?" Sarah asked.

"Oh, come now, Sarah Dawson, we've all had a go at it. She's tried us, every one. And the little beggar manages to get what she wants out of each and every one of us. Poor child. She wants only to live a normal life. You'll never figure out the riddle. It makes no sense at all. It's just a child's game."

"You may be a lieutenant in McClellan's bodyguard but you don't know everything," Sarah flung at him. She was disappointed that she wasn't the sole beneficiary of the riddle. And angry. She knew her response was childish, the kind she'd give to her sister Betsy. And she was ashamed of it. Kate would handle this differently, she was sure of it. Kate would put him in his place. But she was not entirely sure she wanted to put him in his place.

He knelt down beside her, both hands holding the rifle upright. "I'm your friend, Sarah Dawson, if that is indeed your name. I would be honored to be considered your friend."

"And why shouldn't it be my name?"

"Because nobody is what they seem here in this house. Everybody is hiding something. Nobody is what they were in Washington before the war came. And what they are now, they won't be anymore when the war is over."

Her thoughts exactly, put into words by someone else. "That sounds like a riddle." She sat up, and returned his level brown gaze.

"Who are you?" he asked.

"If I'm anybody else than I've claimed to be, why would I tell you?"

"You shouldn't. But I wish to be your friend."

"Why?"

"Because something tells me you need one."

His voice was husky and low, and Sarah felt the words

grace her heart. Too close, she decided, too close. This is one of the problems Kate did warn me about. Sheldon, cock of the rock. If he is on Rose's side, he is exactly the one to give me away. Still, there was something so sincere about the young man. And his words rang so true. She did need a friend. Since leaving Doctor Hammond's employ, she'd been lonely.

"I can help you figure the riddle out. If you find the diary, what would you do with it? You'd have to give it to me, wouldn't you?"

"I'm not looking for a diary," she lied.

"I like you," he said. "So I'm going to give you what I've already learned about the riddle. Then you can decide if you want to confide in me. How is that?"

"I have nothing to confide," she said.

"You're good at what you do, no matter who you're doing it for. Now listen to this. When you read the riddle, try not to take it at face value. What I mean is, some words have two spellings, or it could be a coded message. Rose, the mother, is very good at that. Did you ever think she had Little Rose approach you, just to throw you off track and test you?"

Sarah hadn't. And she was grateful to him for his help, but she couldn't let him know that. "I'm tired of the whole thing," she said. "Like you said, it's a child's game." And to show him she meant it, she ripped up the paper with the riddle right in front of him.

Of course, she'd memorized it. Papers were always better memorized then destroyed. Kate had told her that. Rose herself had eaten a piece of paper with a message printed on it the night Pinkerton came to her door with one of his men to arrest her.

And then, with all the sand of Lily Mackall, Sarah stood up, held her head high, and started for the back door of the house.

"Did you ever think that maybe the word *stare* has a different spelling?"

She stopped.

"As in stairway? Or stairs?"

She turned.

He stood up and walked toward her. "Look, I think I know what you're about here, but you don't have to tell me if it would compromise your position. Do what you promised the little girl to keep her quiet, then consider the word *s-t-a-i-r*. I have a feeling the diary is under one of the stairs. Trust me and we'll find it together."

Sarah felt her heart beating rapidly. He was whispering to her. His eyes were warm and appealing. "Why do you pander to her so?" she asked.

"For the same reason you do. And everyone does. She's

powerful. I can guarantee you she's still going to try to run secrets out of this house. If you are who I think you are, watch Lily Mackall. She's the liaison. Sometimes Rose and her daughter are allowed to go out for a walk with the guards. That's usually in the cool of the evening. If you decide to trust me, I'll stay at home this evening and we'll investigate the stairs. I'll tell the other guards to keep her out about an hour. What do you say?"

"And if a diary is found?"

"I'll let you have it," he said.

Sarah knew what she must do. "I think with the rest of my hour I'll walk to the confectioner's and get an ice cream," she said. "Then I'll let you know."

"Fine," he said. "I'll walk you to the front gate."

CHAPTER SEVENTEEN

August 28, Fort Greenhow, Washington

SARAH WENT IMMEDIATELY DOWN THE TREE-SHADED street to the confectioner's, hoping the woman named Iris would be there. She'd been told that to make the contact she must ask for some gingerbread. Iced. That was the password.

Only one other customer was there. It was dinnertime in Washington. Sarah waited until he got his purchases wrapped and left. The woman behind the counter was small and wore her hair in a bun. She must be Iris, Sarah thought, but I must be sure.

"I'd like some gingerbread," she said.

Through spectacles the woman narrowed her eyes and took Sarah's measure. "Yes?"

"Iced," Sarah said. "It must be iced."

She nodded and went into a back room, and Sarah had a brief moment of panic. Suppose she could not be trusted and had gone to fetch someone who would then know her as a Pinkerton spy? Would she be arrested and sent over Rebel lines? She closed her eyes and told herself, sternly, to stop it. The woman soon came back with the cake, wrapped it, and handed it to Sarah, who paid her and smiled.

"You are Sarah, then."

"Yes."

"How can I help you today?"

"Sheldon, head of the Sturgis Rifles, suspects who I am and asked me to trust him. I must obtain advice."

She nodded. "A box of cake will come around for you in about an hour. Say you ordered it for Rose. In the cake will be a piece of paper with the answer. Destroy it immediately."

"Thank you." Sarah rushed from the shop. An hour. That would be well before the evening came, before Rose went on her walk. She felt easier in her mind, and hoped the answer that came back would be in the affirmative. She found herself hoping she would be allowed to trust Sheldon.

To Sarah's surprise, there was another guest in the house when she returned. A woman, short, squat, dark-haired, with a clear complexion and a determined jaw, stood at the bottom of the stairway, looking up. Next to her was Lieutenant Sheldon.

At their feet, and on the stairway, were strewn clothing and an open portmanteau, even toilet articles. At the top of the stairs, looking down, was Rose Greenhow, her little daughter beside her.

"I'll not have her in Gertrude's room. How dare you put her in Gertrude's room?" She was shaking.

"I'm sorry, Mrs. Greenhow," Lieutenant Sheldon said. "I did not approve it."

"Well, you aren't doing your job if you're not controlling your subordinates," she near screamed at him. "I do not even want her in the house with me! It might have been supposed that my former social position, and that which members of my immediately family still hold in the Federal City, would have protected me from this attempt to degrade me."

"There was no intent to degrade you, Mrs. Greenhow."

"And I'll not have her at the table with me, either. I prefer starvation to breaking bread with a woman of the streets!"

"I am not a woman of the streets," the lady in question shouted back.

"Please, both of you," Sheldon begged. "I shall remedy the situation. We all must learn to endure one another here and make the best of a bad situation."

"I shall not endure any more than I have to," Mrs. Greenhow shouted. "And keep her away from my innocent Little Rose! Besides which, she was sent here to spy on me!"

With that, she turned, dragging innocent Little Rose with her. Immediately, the woman who stood next to Sheldon put both hands over her face and started to cry, or at least her shoulders were shaking. Sarah saw that Sheldon did not know what all to do. He was beside himself. "Don't get upset," Sarah implored. "Rose insults everybody."

She found herself disturbed that someone sent to the house as a prisoner should be insulted and have her things thrown about. The woman was not disagreeable-looking, but then neither was she as elegant or pretty as Rose.

Her hands came down from her face then, and Sarah

saw she'd not been crying, but laughing, although it was, in part, a desperate laugh.

"She and I were friends at one time, when my husband was alive. Then he became ill, and she no longer wanted anything to do with me. What has this war done to people? She calls me a woman of the streets! Is she mad? Shouldn't she be in an insane asylum?"

Sheldon said, "Mrs. Onderdonk, this is Sarah Dawson, Rose's maid."

"Medora," she corrected. "Call me Medora."

"Yes, well, perhaps, Sarah, you will help her get settled in the room at the end of the hall? And I am sorry," Sheldon said as the woman bent to retrieve her things.

He took it all upon himself, Sarah minded. He sounded like a considerate host whose guests had started an argument at the table. Sarah helped Medora with her things and brought her upstairs to the small room at the end of the hall. As she settled in, Sarah watched her.

Was she a spy? Sent from Pinkerton?

"I must rest," Medora said, and she slipped off her dress and sat to remove her shoes. "I am not a spy, Miss Dawson. I know what I am. I am not proud of it. Or of what I've had to do to survive, since my husband died. He left me in debt, you see. Afterward, I was befriended by many men. Rose is angry with me, you see, because many of my men friends are also hers. Only she entertained them to get information from them. And I am suspected by the government now and put here, because those men had to do with Rose. I am tainted by the same brush. But if they ever find what they are looking for here, if the names of those men are written down at all anywhere, it will clear me. Until then, I suppose I must stay."

The woman was straightforward, and her manner without self-pity. Sarah thought how much better a person she was than Rose, yet Rose went about queening it up. Sarah decided that she liked her.

She decided that Medora was referring to Rose's diary. Finding it would be the most important thing she could do, she told herself. But she had never before imagined that it would be of help to anyone but the government.

Little less than an hour later the cake came from the confectioner's, delivered by a small Negro boy who reminded Sarah of Nubbin. And, with a pang, she realized how much she missed him. And Doctor Hammond, as well as the simple, uncomplicated life she'd been leading before in the army.

The bag had her name on it and it was to be delivered only to her, the little Negro boy insisted, and so she was summoned to the door by the Sturgis guard and immediately took the cake to the kitchen. No one was there; supper hour was over and Rose was upstairs dressing for her walk with her guards.

She had to cut the cake open in several places before she found the paper. When she took it out, she was surprised at the measure of her disappointment.

"You were told about Sheldon," it said simply. "Trust no one. Give away your position to no one. Do your best." She did not recognize the handwriting.

Alone with the written rebuke, she wanted to cry. She felt slapped.

Trust no one.

She ripped the note into tiny bits and put it into the stove. Rose and Little Rose were coming down the stairs, dressed for their evening stroll. Lily Mackall was with them. Rose nodded to Sarah, and the child happily skipped along. "It will be so good to get out in the air," Rose was saying. "Come along, child. Washington is lovely in the dark."

Sheldon had gone upstairs to see that Medora was still resting. No one else was now in the house. He came back down, removed his coat, undid his cravat, and set them aside. From the kitchen he fetched some tools. Then he and Sarah stood staring at each other.

"Where do we start?" he asked.

"I've been studying on the riddle," Sarah said.

"Yes?"

She repeated the last line softly, giving every word weight. "You'll know my tears make one." Then she put her foot on the first step. "Right here. This one is it. She says one."

Sheldon grinned at her. "That's good," he said, "very good. But," and he hesitated.

"But what?"

"It's too easy. She could mean the first step at the bottom or at the top."

Sarah sighed. "I hadn't given that much thought. Well, we'd best get to work then and try both. But what will we do about the carpet? If Rose sees it's been cut, she'll know."

"We'll go at the step from the sides. It won't touch the carpet. See?" He took her arm and led her to one side of the steps in the hall. "Right here. I'll cut a hole in the wood."

"How?"

"I spent hours watching the carpenter on our plantation," he said.

"You lived on a plantation?"

He blushed. "Yes. In Maryland. But we had no slaves."

He was embarrassed and would say no more about it. He must come from quality, Sarah decided. And he doesn't want to flaunt it. But that would explain the expensive Irish linen shirts. And the gallant manners. And yes, he must have watched someone to learn to do what he did.

First, he tapped the bottom step with his fist, listening to the sound of it. Then he went up to the top step and tapped that. "The bottom doesn't sound as hollow," he said. And he proceeded to drill a hole in the side of the bottom step. "We don't have much time," he said, "but an hour is enough."

Patiently he worked, while Sarah kept watch at the front windows and spoke once to the guard outside the door to make sure he gave them sufficient warning if Rose was seen returning too soon. But Sheldon had given orders to his men to keep her out even longer than an hour if possible. And well before the time was up, he was asking Sarah to come over and kneel down and thrust her hand into the hole he'd made, because it was smaller than his.

She did so, lying on her stomach on the floor, fumbling around inside the step. And then her hand came upon something. "I've got it," she said. "I've got something, anyway. Yes, it feels like leather. A book. It's flexible, but I'll have to try to fold it over to get it out of the hole."

More struggling. Her hand did not have enough leverage, but she kept trying. Finally she managed to fold over the slender leather volume, but pulling it out of the hole was something else. Twice she dropped it and had to get a grip on it again. The third time she managed to bring one end of it through the hole.

It was red leather. It was very good leather.

It was Rose Greenhow's diary.

A thrill went through Sarah as she rifled through it. Here were names, dates, entries. Here were all the secrets of the spy that her government wanted to know. She looked at Sheldon. He gave her an impassive look back.

"Move aside it you want to look. I have to get this step back together."

Sarah closed the book and sat back and watched him work, forming in her mind what she must do next.

All the mess was cleaned up and the tools put away. She stood with Sheldon admiring his finished work.

"I can give it to the provost-marshal, as I'm supposed to do," he said. "Or you can have it to do with what you need to do."

"I was only helping you with your job," she told him. "I have no need of it. I don't need to do anything."

She summoned forth the mettle to meet his brown eyes with all the innocence she could manage. Sarah wasn't a coquette. She never had cause to be. But something inside her, some woman thing, gave her the ability to do it.

"All right then," Sheldon replied, "all right. I'm sorry I accused you of needing it. And I appreciate your help. I'll get this right to the provost-marshal's office."

She felt loathe to let the precious diary go. But there was something more she had to say if she wanted to protect it. "Your men will be so proud of you," she told him.

He gave her a quizzical look and went out the front door. Sarah had protected the diary. She now must get through to her contact that Sheldon had it. And if it was not turned in to the provost-marshal's office he would be in trouble. For his men would know he had it. He'd have to tell them, for she'd hinted she would if he didn't.

He could not destroy the diary if he was working for Rose or the Confederates.

Sarah felt ashamed. This was a dirty, dangerous business. People got hurt, sure as if they'd been hit on the field of battle. How she longed for that battlefield now, for that good, honest confrontation, where you could see your enemy, where you could take aim and fire at them in God's good sunlight.

Look at Medora, once a friend of Rose. Look at what was going on between herself and Sheldon. It was as if they were locked in some dark waltz and the music would not stop.

CHAPTER EIGHTEEN

September 5, Fort Greenhow, Washington

SEPTEMBER IN WASHINGTON WAS WORSE THAN August for the heat, Sarah learned. Many nights, listening to Rose's tossings and turnings, snores and moans, which seemed to indicate she had nightmares, Sarah thought of home in September.

She thought of how the air would be already cool at dusk, with the first maples and beech trees turning. And, midday, the haze of autumn would be on the land. Here summer still sat, like a sweltering mantle.

The day after Sarah and Sheldon discovered Rose's diary was one of unforgiving heat. Everyone was taken with a lassitude. Until Mrs. Phillips came, to distract them, wearing the widest hoopskirt Sarah had ever seen, and accompanied by Fanny, Caroline, and Emma, pretty girls of fourteen, twelve, and ten, dressed all in white with their own miniature hoopskirts. They looked to Sarah like a group of moths fluttering about.

Mrs. Phillips was the wife of a Washington lawyer. She was from Alabama, and her sister, she promptly told everyone, was Phoebe Yates. She let that be known in the first five minutes after her arrival. Sarah had never heard of Phoebe Yates, but soon learned that she ran a hospital in Richmond.

The family filled the house. They made lots of noise. The girls ran up and down the stairs and played the rosewood pianoforte. They demanded their creature comforts, especially Mrs. Philips, who was a handsome woman with hair curled over her forehead and a dimple in her chin.

"I must see my friend, Rose," she told Sheldon as soon as she was in the door. But Sheldon, to Sarah's surprise, said no.

"I'm sorry, I cannot allow that, Mrs. Phillips."

The woman was what Sarah had always imagined a Southern belle to be — by turns flirtatious and conniving.

She stamped her foot at Sheldon. "I insist that you tell Mr. Stanton I am here. I will not stay in this horrid place!"

But somehow Sheldon saw to it that they were settled in anyway. A special order of ice was sent for, as well as lemonade. She demanded mosquito netting around the bedposts, because the windows must be open at night. The softest linens were found for the beds. "At home we have the Negroes fan my girls while they sleep," she complained. "That room is so hot upstairs."

"We're fighting a war, Mrs. Phillips," Sheldon said. "To free Negroes from such servitude." His tone said everything, and Sarah was so proud of him for putting her in her place.

"I thought the Yankees were fighting us to keep us in the Union," she snapped.

"It's over the Negroes, to free them," Sheldon returned quickly. "And if that reason isn't brought to light, it soon will be."

The next morning Mr. Edward Stanton came. Sarah knew he'd been Attorney General, wanted to be Secretary of War, and might soon be appointed as such. How did such a woman as Mrs. Phillips bring the soon-to-be Secretary of War running? Sarah had seen what men could accomplish in her time in the army. Never had she thought women could wield such power. And as always, she thought of her poor mother.

The whole house was in a tizzy with the arrival of Stanton, who strutted about the parlor with self-importance like a bantam rooster. Sarah, as the only maid, was required to serve him tea in the parlor, along with Mrs. Phillips and her daughters. She heard Stanton promising Mrs. Phillips that he would make immediate arrangements for their transportation south.

"In the meantime, Eugenia," he told her, "I'll see to it that everything is done to make your stay here more comfortable."

Rose had told Sarah that Mrs. Phillips had had her papers ransacked, that she was suspected of spying. But though both Rose and Medora were confined to their rooms while the Phillips clan was in the house, Rose defended Mrs. Phillips to Sarah.

"She's no spy. She is a true Southern woman who didn't have the sense to leave this city once the war started. And she won't associate with the mudsills left in this town. And Stanton is a sycophant. And a weakling. Though I must admit, he is a brilliant lawyer."

Rose was jealous, however, of the attention Sarah was required to give the Phillipses, and of the fact that Stanton had come to the house and not asked to see her.

The Phillipses stayed two days. In that time, Sarah was run ragged waiting on them and pacifying Rose and Little

Rose, who became more and more petulant since they were confined to their rooms.

When the Phillipses left in a great fanfare, with a chaise waiting at the curb for them, Rose was just returning from an afternoon walk under the guardianship of Sheldon. Little Caroline broke away from her mother, ran over to Lieutenant Sheldon, and spit on the coat of his spotless uniform.

"That's a nice way to raise your daughters," he called after Mrs. Phillips as she was getting into the chaise. "If women like you are let loose, our lives are in jeopardy."

The beautiful Eugenia Phillips smiled over her shoulder at him as she was helped into the chaise. "We of the South consider all Northerners swine. And we hire butchers to kill our swine," she said.

While all that was going on, Rose took a ball of pink yarn out of her reticule and threw it so it landed on Mrs. Philips's feet. "You left this, Eugenia," Rose said. For just an instant the two women exchanged looks. Emma picked up the yarn, held it for a moment, then gave it to her mother.

Something in the exchange bothered Sarah. Where had Mrs. Phillips left it? She had never seen her knitting, or doing any needlework. All Sarah's instincts told her to demand the ball of yarn, but she could not rush forward without giving herself away.

Never was she so glad to see anybody leave. But it was only after the Phillipses departed and Rose was allowed out of her room again that she discovered that the first step had been tampered with.

Sarah was in the kitchen when the shrieking began. Rose dropped a glass of water on the floor and it echoed in the house. "My diary! Who has been at this step! Who has dared rip apart my house?"

Sarah went running. In the hall Rose was throwing things about, newspapers, books, even the umbrellas in the stand.

"Did you take my diary?" she demanded. Her face was red, her chin trembled, even her hands were shaking. Little Rose appeared from upstairs and sat on the top step, watching.

"I don't know of any diary," Sarah responded firmly.

"Look what they've done to the beautiful wood of my staircase," Rose said, pointing. "It's all scratched. It's been violated and not even put back together properly!"

"What has the stair to do with your diary?" Sarah asked innocently.

Rose ignored her. "Sheldon, oh, dear Lieutenant Sheldon, did you do this to me?" Now the voice was plaintive, pitiful.

Sheldon drew himself up straight. "I didn't want to, Rose. I was under orders."

"Whose orders? Oh, I know. It was that Stanton, wasn't it? He wants to be Secretary of War so badly. And he thinks to make himself inroads with Lincoln by producing my diary! But how did he know? Tell me, Sheldon," and she lowered her voice to an indulgent tone. "I know you only do as you're told, just tell me. How did they know to look here?"

"I don't know, Ma'am, except that they've looked everywhere else."

"And when was this done, then?"

"When you were out the other day, walking."

"And where is my precious diary now?"

"I don't know, Ma'am," Sheldon lied. "I was obliged to turn it over to the authorities."

"Oh, I must sit down," Rose wailed. "I feel faint."

Out of the corner of her eye Sarah saw Little Rose scramble back upstairs, like a bird in flight, from the sight of her mother being led over to a chair. Sheldon produced a bottle of whiskey and offered her a small glass.

"Oh," she said sarcastically, "whiskey. The masculine panacea for all the ills of life." But she drank it and allowed herself to be pacified by Sheldon.

Sarah went upstairs to find Little Rose.

✦ ✦ ✦

At this moment in the madness of those early September days, Sarah knew two things to be true: first, that she had some currency with Little Rose, for as she'd promised, she'd asked for and received permission that the child be allowed to attend her party. Rose had agreed a week ago, as long as Sheldon accompanied her. And he had.

And she knew that Little Rose was afraid of her mother. She'd indicated as much to Sheldon on the walk to and from the elegant house two blocks away.

"Mama demands total loyalty," the child had told him.

Sarah did not know if Little Rose even understood the phrase. She doubted if she understood it herself. Or if she had, she was undergoing a sea change in her former comprehension of things. It seemed that all the truths that had held through all of her life were up for questioning. And they did not fit into the pattern of the manners and morals of the house on Sixteenth Street that went by the name of Fort Greenhow.

Little Rose was on her bed in her room, white and trembling, as Sarah had supposed she would be. She held the doll Sarah had brought her that first day.

"Your mama will be fine, don't worry," Sarah told her.

The child looked up at her with saucer eyes. "Did you find my mama's diary?"

"No," Sarah lied.

"I don't believe you."

"Believe what you wish. I wouldn't believe me, either. If I were in your situation I wouldn't believe anybody," Sarah said. She sat down on the bed next to Little Rose.

"You kept your promise. I got to go to the party," Little Rose argued.

Sarah shrugged. "I thought you should be allowed to go. You're cooped up in here all week. It isn't natural. Why would I want to do this to your mama? Think on it. Because of her I have a job. I didn't have one before. I want to stay here with you and her. It's a good job."

"Are you poor?"

"Compared to almost everybody in Washington, yes. I have no means of income. I must support myself."

"What did you think of my riddle, then?"

"I think it was very clever. And that you're a very smart little girl. Too smart to let yourself get embroiled in all of this going on around here. It isn't your affair or your worry. It's your mama's."

"Do you think you could have figured out where the diary was from the riddle?"

"No. I was concentrating on the veils. I thought you were referring to curtains. If I'd been looking for it, I would have looked around curtains."

Little Rose giggled. "I had you fooled."

"Yes, you did. But I'm not very clever, Rose, that's why I'm only a maid."

The child nodded solemnly. "You may be only a maid, but I wish I were you."

"Oh? Why?"

"Because Sheldon's sweet on you. He told me."

Sarah blushed. "That's nonsense."

"Yes, he is! I wish he was sweet on me. I think he's so handsome! Don't you?"

"Yes."

Little Rose sighed. "I wish I could grow up faster. And this war was over."

"We all wish the war was over, Rose. It's nasty, and it turns people against each other."

"But it makes people meet each other, too. Like you and Sheldon." She giggled again. "Would you marry him?"

"Marry?" Sarah brushed a stray curl off the little round face. "He'd never ask. He's from quality and I'm from a poor farm family."

"My mama says the war is going to do away with all the old distinctions. That there will be no proper order of things anymore. That Negroes will be marrying whites. If that happens, why couldn't you marry Sheldon?"

Sarah put her arm around the child and drew her close.

"I'm not sure the war will do that. It's up to us, as individuals, if we want things to change."

"I want things to change and I don't," Little Rose confided. "Sometimes I get afraid. Are you ever afraid?"

"Yes," Sarah admitted. "Now you know what? I'd like to buy you a present. I get a salary, and we're true friends. And I want to buy you something. What would you like, a new dolly?"

"No." Rose pulled away. "I'd like a Noah's ark. Adele got one for her birthday at the party. It's got two of all the animals. Little wooden ones. And a Noah. It's so cunning!"

"Then I'll find one for you," Sarah promised.

"This house is like an ark, isn't it?" Little Rose asked then. "Did you ever think that? We're all in here together and sometimes we fight like animals. Only there's no flood outside."

Oh, yes, there is, Sarah thought, even as she marveled at the child's insights. Oh, yes, there is a flood outside. And I feel the waters, rising and rising and rising.

"You know what I think, Sarah? I think that when God made all those animals, He was practicing. He made them all different shapes and sizes, and He just kept on practicing. For when He made man. But He had to practice a lot, first. That's why the animals are all so different-looking. What do you think?"

"Sometimes," Sarah said, "I think He didn't practice enough."

September 8, Fort Greenhow, Washington

"Did you hear?" Medora Onderdonk stuck her head out of her bedroom door. "Did you hear that the war is over slavery? I knew it all the time."

"Slavery?" Sarah paused on her way to Rose's room. Rose had a headache, and no wonder. All of Washington was buzzing about her diary. Well, Sheldon had always said the real reason for the war would soon come to light. But what had happened for Medora to say this?

"That Fremont fellow," Medora explained, "is freeing the slaves in Missouri. It's your home state, isn't it?"

That Fremont fellow, Sarah knew from Sheldon, commanded the army in the West. She'd learned a lot from Sheldon; otherwise, living here in Fort Greenhow, which was like being on a desert island, she'd have no news of the war at all. There was no news to be had, really. Neither army had done anything all summer.

She had to remind herself that Missouri was supposed to be her state. Her own lying, so necessary to the job, was likely to trip her up one of these days. "I've had no letters from home. But is it true? Fremont has freed the slaves? By what right?"

"That's what I want to know. If Rose wasn't so tied up in her own worries, she'd be having a hissy-fit over it. She always said that's what the war was about and not states' rights. Now Lincoln will have to admit it. How is she?"

"Not too well today," Sarah said. "I'm on my way to her now to bring her a powder for her headache."

"I would think she wouldn't be too well. My Lord, I can hear the newsboys on the streets yelling her name from my window."

Sarah had heard them, too, and with each yell was reminded of her own hand in the affair.

It was terrible. Rose's life was laid bare in the newspapers. And the lives of many other important men in Washington. Rose's agents were in the diary, too. Many lives in Washington and out of it were ruined this day, not only statesmen, but lawyers, bankers, cotton brokers, soldiers, and government clerks. The diplomatic corps, too.

And worst of all, some of these people had gotten notes from Rose to warn them beforehand and had been able to flee. Others were even now, as Sarah brought the powder and lemonade to Rose's room, being arrested.

Sarah felt guilty because of the warnings that had been smuggled out of the house. Somehow it was her fault. How could Rose be sending messages? She'd seemed busy all the time, especially since Sheldon had gotten her back her sewing machine and her tapestry.

Sarah did not want to listen to the little nagging voice inside her head, or what it was saying, of course.

It was saying *Lieutenant Sheldon.* Twice she'd seen him accepting papers from Rose and putting them in his pocket.

Rose had taken to teasing them all of late, saying she had "a little bird" to help her, and they would never stop her communications.

Was Sheldon her "little bird"? Sarah couldn't bear thinking on it. And it had nothing to do with the fact that she knew she was smitten with him. Nothing at all, she kept telling herself. It had to do with the fact that she thought him trustworthy.

Then, on top of all that, Sheldon had told her this morning as she was bringing Rose her breakfast that he'd had word that when Mrs. Phillips left, she'd smuggled a message from Rose to Jeff Davis in Richmond. Pinkerton's man in Richmond had gotten word back to him.

Sarah had stopped dead in her tracks. "The ball of pink yarn," she'd told him. "I knew it. I saw the look between them when Rose threw it at Mrs. Phillips." She didn't add that she wanted to run forward and take it.

"Why didn't you tell me?" Sheldon had been clearly upset.

"I helped you once," Sarah said. "Finding the diary. I'm Rose's maid. I have no other reason for being here. I told you that."

Still, Sheldon did not believe her. And it grieved her that she had to lie to him. She'd watched him go down the walk on his way to the provost-marshal's office, so handsome in his uniform, his sword officially at his side. He was going to be called to account for the messages that had gone out of the house. She just knew it.

It was so tiresome for Sarah, having to keep up the charade with him. If only her superiors would give her permission to confide in him, they could work together. But then there would be more chance that Rose would know who she was. And being loyal to Rose at this point was more important for the cause than anything. Because somebody had to stay close enough to her to find out how she was getting messages out.

Sarah didn't know how much longer she could keep up this spy business. One spy spying on another was what it was. Everybody double-dealing. She hadn't been brought up that way. She'd been brought up to honest toil. You planted, you cared for animals, and in turn the earth and the animals gave back to you. And if the rains came too often, or not enough, or the animals took sick and died, you blamed God and took your losses and started over again. But there was no treachery, no evil, no greed involved. That was the contract when you farmed, and there was no fine print, no person in the middle to jumble things up.

She trudged wearily down the hall to Rose's room and Medora went down to give Little Rose her morning piano lesson. Somewhere in her distant past, the solid, unaffected Medora had been taught to play. And Sheldon had given permission for her to give Little Rose lessons of a morning. It kept them both occupied.

Rose was near prostration as Sarah entered the room. The green paper shades were drawn and she lay on the bed in her ruffled undergarments. "They're going to arrest the mayor of Washington," she was moaning. "He'll be sent to prison. Oh, I feel so sorry for all these people."

By now Sarah knew Rose well enough to know she felt sorry only for herself. "I've brought your headache powder," she said.

Rose sat up. "Is my daughter all right?"

"Yes. Medora is giving her piano lessons right now. Can't you hear?"

Rose had objected to the lessons at first. "I don't want my daughter taught anything by that woman of the streets!" she'd told Sheldon. But he'd talked her into it, saying how good it was for Little Rose. And how gentle Medora was with her.

"She'll turn my daughter against me," Rose had whined.

Sheldon said he'd given Medora stern instructions never to speak badly of Rose, and that Little Rose was to come to him if she did. That pacified Rose. Sarah didn't know how Sheldon did it, keeping the two women from each other's throats, keeping Rose's feathers unruffled. But he did.

"If Medora tells her anything of this scandal with my diary, I'll kill her," Rose threatened. "I want her touched by none of this," Rose said. "I want none of my children touched."

Well, then, Sarah thought, you might have considered that before you became part of a spy ring that extends from Boston to New Orleans, as the papers are saying.

"I'm worse than Marie Antoinette," she told Sarah, "when they snatched a letter from that poor queen's bosom. My deepest secrets have been snatched from my bosom. Where is Sheldon? I need his kind concern at this moment."

"Summoned to his superiors."

"Is he under suspicion?"

"No. Why should he be?"

"Because he's been so good to me. That young man has made my life here bearable."

How bearable? Sarah wondered darkly. Every time Rose spoke of Sheldon it was in special tones. And every time it grated on Sarah's nerves. Because her tone and manner intimated a romantic interest that Sheldon had in her. Of course, she reminded herself, Rose thinks every man has a romantic interest in her. But still, it was possible. Oh, no, she reminded herself sternly, don't think that way, don't. Stop thinking altogether, Sarah Wheelock. This place is making you crazy.

CHAPTER NINETEEN

September 10, Fort Greenhow, Washington

SHELDON DID NOT COME BACK FOR TWO DAYS, AND everyone was without word of him at all, and very worried. Sarah thought Rose would go out of her mind missing him and wondering what new attack the government would take upon her. She considered Sheldon her own protection.

Sarah was scarcely managing to stay sane herself. One moment she would think, "Sheldon's been placed under arrest. He's part of Rose's conspiracy." And the next she'd tell herself, "He's going through planning sessions. They're figuring ways to keep Rose from sending out more messages."

She felt isolated, more alone even than back on the farm when she'd had a fight with Betsy over some trifling thing and had no one but Ma to talk to. And Ma wasn't talking.

She longed to visit Doctor Hammond. Oh, how she needed a friend! But to ask permission would be to admit weakness. And she wasn't supposed to contact him anyway.

And then, on the second morning of Sheldon's absence the little Negro boy from the confectioner's appeared at the door once again with a cake for Sarah.

Quickly she took it into the kitchen and when she was sure she was alone, knifed into it and drew out the message.

"Timothy Webster has been hanged for espionage in Richmond," it said. "Be careful. Greenhow has power."

Timothy Webster! One of Pinkerton's most skilled operatives! Sarah's hands trembled as she ripped up the note. The news, and lack of details, plunged her into a deep despair. Yet it was what she needed at the moment. It made her know, surely, that she was alone. All spies were. And if you were caught, no one stepped forward to help you.

How different is that from my life at home? she asked herself. I was alone there. Ma could never help me. That life prepared me for this. If I want to put any meaning on that life and all its unhappiness, and deem it worth anything, I must take lessons from it.

That afternoon two new women prisoners arrived and, with Sheldon gone, nobody was there to take charge. Sergeant Mark Stevens of the Sturgis Rifles looked to Sarah to settle them in. "Just do the best you can until Sheldon gets back," he advised. "Call if you need help."

One prisoner was named Catherine Virginia Baxley, and the other would be known only as Mrs. Poole.

Mrs. Baxley was fifty years old, but looked younger than Sarah's mother. She came in waving a paper. "I have here a letter for Rose Greenhow from President Jeff Davis. And a bag of nuts from his dining table." She waved the bag under Sarah's nose. "I bring these nuts because Rose knows what President Davis's tastes are in food, and she knows he loves these."

Sarah's first impulse was to take the letter, but that would give her away. So she turned to the task at hand. Rose was on the stairway. Behind her were Little Rose, Medora, and Lizzy Fitzgerald, the child's nurse.

Mrs. Poole, tall and thin, wearing black and spectacles, commenced yelling, "I'll not stay in this place! I'll not take one bit of food given by the Yankee government! I'll starve!"

"Give me my letter," Rose demanded, coming down the stairs and thrusting out her hand.

"First, say it," Catherine Virginia deemed. "Are these not the nuts President Davis prefers?"

Rose pushed the nuts aside roughly. The bag fell to the floor and they rolled in all directions.

"Look what you've done! Look what you've done to the nuts President Davis sent you! Have you no respect? You'll not get the letter until you pick them up! Get down on your knees and pick them up!" Catherine Virginia yelled.

"I'll not sleep under one blanket provided by the Yankee government!" Mrs. Poole was screaming. "Not one!"

Then Rose and Catherine Virginia were tussling over the letter. They were slapping each other. Sarah knew this was beyond her abilities, and was about to reach for the front doorknob when it opened and Sergeant Stevens stood there. He was very well built, with red hair and blazing blue eyes.

"Quiet!" he boomed. "What's all this fussing? You're like a bunch of hens! Quiet, or I'll lock you all in your rooms!"

"You haven't the authority!" Rose turned from Catherine Virginia and screamed it in young Stevens's face.

Immediately he held his rifle at a slant in front of him, warning her off. "Try it, lady," he told her in an icy tone that even put Sarah on notice. "I don't care how important you think you are. Try questioning my authority."

Rose started to cry then. All of them did. Sarah found herself surrounded by bawling women. Little Rose came down the stairs and ran to her mother to encircle her waist with her arms.

"I want Lieutenant Sheldon," Rose wailed. "He's the only one who knows how to settle me. He'd give me whiskey now, he would."

"You'll get no whiskey from me!" Stevens said. "Nor coddling, either. Sarah here's been a good friend to you, waiting on you hand and foot. And now she's got herself a henhouse of women all demanding and troublesome. Is that all you think of her?"

Rose brought herself under control. She stopped crying and looked at Stevens over the handkerchief she held to her face. "All right, I'll behave," she said. "For you."

Sarah was amazed. How could a woman who wielded such power turn, in one instant, into a little girl?

Stevens stayed in the house from then on, posting another man at the door. He helped Sarah settle all the women into their rooms. Sarah was grateful to him. Especially when supper was delivered and Mrs. Poole threw her food on the floor.

"I'll not eat any food supplied by the Yankee government," she said.

"Then you'll starve," Stevens told her. But he wouldn't let Sarah clean up the mess. Or Medora, who offered to do it. He made Mrs. Poole get buckets of water and rags and he stood over her until the floor in her room was spotless again.

He had his work cut out for him. Rose pushed her way into the room to rant and rave at Mrs. Poole for destroying her good hardwood floors. Stevens made her leave. He ordered her out, and she obeyed him.

Sarah was beginning to think he should be the head of the Sturgis Rifles. We wouldn't be in the mess we're in now if he was, she decided, with Rose still sneaking out messages.

That evening when she brought a blanket to Mrs. Poole, the woman threw it at her. "It's stamped U.S. Can't you see it? How can I sleep under a blanket stamped like that?" she asked.

In that moment Sarah determined that the poor woman was demented. The war had done it, she decided. Someday, if I don't mind myself, I'll be like that. A person has to be strong in life. A person must practice strength, even if they don't feel it.

Who had said that to her?

With dismay, Sarah recalled it had been her father.

Never mind: He must have gotten it from somebody else, she told herself. Then she stood, straight and proud. "You may not wish to have this blanket, Mrs. Poole, but you will pick it up and hand it back to me." She used her most severe tone, the one she'd used on Ezekiel Kunkle. Mrs. Poole bent to pick up the blanket, and for a moment Sarah felt triumphant. But, no, she wasn't picking it up, she was falling. Thump, she collapsed right onto the floor.

Mrs. Poole had fainted.

"Sergeant Stevens!" Sarah, all thought of strength deserting her, went running, and the young sergeant came up the stairs with bayonet fixed. "Mrs. Poole has fainted!"

He set his rifle aside in disgust, picked up Mrs. Poole, sat her in a chair, and sent Sarah for water and cold cloths for her head. Then he and Sarah helped her to the bed. "I'll stay and watch," he said. "You go about your business. Sometimes this is a ruse to make the guards think they are helpless."

Sarah thanked him and ran from the room. She'd heard Sheldon's voice downstairs, she was sure of it.

Sheldon came in with a bouquet of late summer roses. He handed them to Sarah.

"Shall I put them in Rose's room?" she asked.

"They're for you," he said. "These are for Rose." He handed a bag to Sarah. "Yarn."

The roses were wrapped in brown paper at the stems. Sarah stood speechless. "Why are the roses for me? And why more yarn for Rose, who uses it to send messages?"

"So we can find out how she does it," he answered. "But is that what you say when a young man gives you flowers, Sarah?"

She thought of the wildflowers that day so long ago now, in Ezekiel Kunkle's one hand, and the knife he held in the other with which he threatened to slash her face. And she did not answer.

Sheldon stripped off his white gloves and undid the top button of his tunic. "They're for you because I like you. And because you helped me that day with the diary. I've been promoted." He grinned at her with that grin that tore Sarah's heart open. "I'm a captain now, Miss Dawson. And you will kindly address me as one."

Sarah could not believe it. "Promoted?" she croaked.

"Yes."

"Because you turned in the diary?"

"In part."

Sarah was not only surprised, she was put out. She herself had received nothing, not even word from her superiors for her work in finding the diary. Neither from Pinkerton nor from Kate. She swallowed her jealousy, but tears came to her eyes at the injustice of it.

"Of course, I told them your part in it," he said, as if reading her thoughts. "I told them I couldn't have done it without you. And that you should be rewarded somehow, but, quite honestly, they do not trust you, Sarah. They think you might truly be working for Rose."

They, of course, was the provost-marshal's office. Didn't these government agencies work together? Sarah wondered. Or is Sheldon just saying that to make me reveal myself? Or maybe they did work together, only weren't telling Sheldon who she was.

And what about the notes she'd seen Sheldon take from Rose and put in his pocket? Was he working for Rose and blaming the messages Rose sneaked out on Sarah?

"I'm sorry, Sarah." Sheldon put his hand on her shoulder, gently. His touch was like the branding of a hot poker to her, yet at the same time she felt chilled. "I wanted to give you credit. And I shall before this is over, I promise. But it would be a lot easier if you were honest with me. And you haven't been, you know."

So that was it. He was still fishing. Sarah swallowed her tears, and took the flowers into the kitchen to find a vase.

✦ ✦ ✦

She brought the yarn upstairs to Rose. "Sheldon brought it. For your tapestry."

A large piece of tapestry, half finished, was stretched on a frame in the corner. It was a hunting scene from the South. Rose did beautiful needlework. Sarah had to give her that.

"Dear boy," Rose said. "I'm going to send this to a friend of mine."

"Who?" Sarah asked distractedly.

"Oh," Rose said lightly, "someone down South. Not the same friend I sent the bookmark to, though. That was just a small piece. You saw it. I sent that to another friend in the South. This is much more detailed."

Sarah had been setting the vase on a Duncan Phyfe table in the corner. And it was then that she was struck with a thought so brilliant, so far-fetched, that she thought lightning had come into the room. She stood up straight and managed to arrange her face in a friendly smile.

"Your work is beautiful," she said. She remembered the bookmark, then. A Sturgis Guard had taken it out for mailing. When was that? *After Rose discovered her diary had been taken, that's when.*

Carelessly, she wandered over to the tapestry on the stand. "This is very detailed," she agreed.

"Yes," Rose said, "and now thanks to Sheldon I can put more colors in this, as it calls for. The bookmark had only red, green, and yellow. I told Sheldon what colors I wanted and he purchased them for me. That's why I like him."

"So many more colors," Sarah commented. She scowled. Something in her mind was just eluding her, like the fox depicted in the tapestry eluded the hounds.

"But, of course. It is like a work of art, tapestry. Like a fine painting that means different things to different people. And I consider myself the artist."

"You are that," Sarah said. "You are that. I have to give you credit, Ma'am."

"Are those dreadful new ladies quiet now?"

"Yes, they've gone to sleep. Sheldon gave them some whiskey."

Rose laughed. "I have a headache from their carrying on. Mark my words. Catherine Virginia will rave from morning to night and drive you all mad. The letter wasn't from Jefferson Davis. Here, take a look at it yourself, it's from an old friend in Richmond. Completely harmless."

Sarah took the letter and scanned it. It did seem harmless. The woman was saying how scarce shoe leather already was in Richmond. Could Rose send her a pair of shoes for her ten-year-old? Of course, Sarah minded, it could be in code.

Code. Yes. That's what spies used. Kate had told her. She felt elation, so much that it made her head dizzy.

"She's a nonentity, that Catherine Virginia," Rose was saying. "She wants to seem important."

"She's been accused of sending two hundred guns south."

"Piffle," Rose said. "They'll both take the oath of allegiance to the United States and be out of here in two days. Mark my words."

A clock downstairs struck the hour ten. "You'd best get some sleep," Sarah advised Rose. "Here, I'll turn back your bed. There's dark clouds on the horizon. I think we'll have rain this night."

"Good," Rose said. "Maybe the air will finally clear."

It's cleared already, Sarah thought, as she helped Rose out of her dress and brought over her silken robe. Oh, you don't know how clear the air has suddenly become.

Then, on the pretense of fetching herself a cup of tea before bed, and coming right back, she asked Rose if she wanted any. The answer was no. Sarah, filled with exultation at what she had just discovered, could scarce keep herself from running from the room.

CHAPTER TWENTY

September 11, Fort Greenhow, Washington

EARLY THE NEXT MORNING, BEFORE ANYONE WAS UP, Sarah knocked softly on the inside of the door of Rose's room. She had an agreement with the guard. Two sharp raps and then one more, and he would know she needed to slip out for something. Thank heavens, she thought as she went out the front door, that once Rose settles down after her tossing and turning, she sleeps heavily.

Outside, in the mist from the Potomac that seemed to muffle every sound and at the same time carry it distinctly on the air, she found Captain Sheldon directing his men in a morning drill. Their footsteps tattooed a muffled rhythm on the cobblestoned street. Seeing her, Sheldon ordered them "at ease" and came running over.

"Where are you off to?"

"I couldn't sleep. The confectioner's. Do you want anything?"

"No. But I did want to ask you to come out walking with me this afternoon when you get your time off. Maybe we can get some ice cream."

Sarah was startled, but quickly said yes. "I'd like that." She was in such a state of excitement at what she'd discovered last evening about the tapestry that she loved all the world this morning. In spite of that, she was determined not to tell Sheldon of her discovery. This bit of information was all her own.

As she walked along the morning streets, skirting a gaggle of geese, horses pulling delivery wagons clopped by her on the cobbled pavement. A morning church bell tolled. Smart-looking carriages went by her, pulled by sleek horses, and she knew they would turn in the front drive of the White House just two blocks ahead. The President rose early, Sarah had heard from some. Others said he never slept, and that he ate only apples, and that Mrs. Lincoln was already famous for her elaborate parties and her visiting Southern relatives and for spending enormous amounts of money on frippery.

She found it hard to believe that the intelligence she was about to give over to Iris in the confectioner's might help President Lincoln himself. That sometime in the next day or two an aide might tell him: "Mr. President, we've received word from Pinkerton. One of his spies has discovered that Mrs. Greenhow sends messages to the South by way of her tapestry."

What would her father say if he knew, he who had called her a dunderhead when he wasn't calling her stupid?

Fish and oyster peddlers went by in their wagons, calling out for customers. Sarah knew that the price of fish had risen drastically because Rebel batteries practicing on the Potomac had frightened off the fishermen and ruined their nets.

In her reticule she now had paper money. Gold and silver coins were fast being driven from circulation. "Secretary Chase's greenbacks," the money was being called. And markets were refusing to give change on them for any purchase less than sixty cents.

Sarah went into the confectioner's. They were just opening up and she was the first customer. Good. "May I help you?" the man behind the counter asked.

The smell of freshly baked bread filled Sarah's nose and

made her hungry. "Yes, I'd like some cinnamon buns," she told him, "but first, I'd like to see Iris."

On her way home the newsboys were out, waving copies of the *Daily Chronicle*. Sarah paid no mind to them at first, then did.

It was something about the Rebel Woman Spy. And a letter. She gave the newsboy one of Secretary Chase's greenbacks, not expecting change, and scanned the front page.

Rose Greenhow had sent a letter to Mr. Seward, which, the paper said, had "somehow been smuggled out of her mansion where she was a prisoner, and was soon to be published in both the *New York Herald* and the *Richmond Whig*, to the embarrassment of President Lincoln."

Sarah ran all the way back to the house on Sixteenth Street. Breathlessly, she ran up the steps, inside, and again up more steps to Rose's room.

"What have you done?" she asked.

"Where were you?" Rose turned from her dressing table, where she sat in her silken robe. "I wanted you to comb out my hair for me."

Sarah remembered that she must act like a maid, that if she were indignant it must be because she was Rose's maid, and for no other reason. Well, on that account she had reason enough to be indignant. "It says in the *Chronicle* that you have to change your clothing within sight of your brutal male captors. That you have had rough handling. That there is general indecency in this house as well as drunken brawling. Oh, how can you! We've all treated you with such consideration."

Rose got up from her dressing-table stool and came to take the bag of cinnamon buns from Sarah's hands. "My, these smell wonderful. Did you get them for me?" Her voice purred.

Sarah shook the newspaper in her face. "Why did you write such lies about us?"

"My dear, I am so sorry," Rose said, "but I had to. I must get the attention of those in power. What I must do is lash out at the statesmen who have been my friends and have now turned against me. Do you think I will be able to do that by telling the world that you get up early in the morning to fetch me cinnamon buns? And that Lieutenant Sheldon gets me yarn? And becalms my nerves with whiskey?"

Sarah sat down on a nearby chair, her breath spent. "I think you are hateful," she said.

"I know you do." Now it was Rose's turn to soothe her. "And I am sorry. I know I owe both you and Captain Sheldon an apology. And I tender it most humbly. But you do understand, child, I must do this. And it will bring results. You will see."

"Sarah, you've got to get away from that house." Captain Sheldon looked across the table at her in Thompson's Drugstore, the very place she had first met Kate Warne so long ago now.

Was it that long ago? No. A month? Six weeks? She felt so much older than when she'd left the army. She knew her way around Washington now, at least this part of it. And she was able to discuss the events of Washington.

Along with everybody else she wondered if President Lincoln was going to nullify the emancipation of slaves that Fremont had freed in the West. And how long General Winfield Scott, who was older than the Constitution, would be in command of the Union army. Or if Mrs. Lincoln's visiting relatives really were smuggling secrets to the South.

She was, in many ways, proud of herself. The old Sarah, the one who slopped her father's hogs back in Michigan, who shot Ezekiel Kunkle's hat off, would never have concerned herself with events in their small town, let alone the country. Now she could discuss with the best of them how President Lincoln had said it would be good to have God on his side, but he must have Kentucky.

Sheldon was still gazing at her across the table. Only now his look had intensified and Sarah sensed that something was coming. "Why do I have to get out of that house?" she asked.

"Because you look wan. And thin. And nervous. And you weren't like that when you first came here. And there's evil in that house." He blushed. "Sarah, do you believe in evil?"

Sarah thought of her father, of the way he knocked her mother about sometimes, and knew she did. "Yes," she said.

"Well, it's there, in that house. You can almost smell it sometimes. And I care about you, Sarah. Surely you know that by now." He reached out his hand and touched hers on the table.

Sarah blushed. She had wanted to hear those words from him, dreamed about hearing them. And now that they were said, she wished they hadn't been. She was not the kind of girl to enjoy his discomfort, to play with his feelings. She believed in honesty between people, especially between men and women. She did not withdraw her hand. That would be rude, by her standards. Her feelings for Captain Sheldon confused her so! When she was with him, she was happy, she knew that. Happier than she'd ever been. And the world, all around her, was painted in brighter strokes so she appreciated the sights and sounds and smells. It was as if she'd been blind, deaf, and dumb before. And now she'd been given all her senses.

Yet, she knew enough not to trust such feelings. Sarah had never wanted to be one of those young women who languished over a man, who made him the whole center of her world, whose every thought was aimed to please him. Even at home in Michigan she'd considered such girls foolish.

Here she was, sitting in an ice-cream parlor and nearly holding hands with a man who made her heart run fast, who made her head whirl. Here she was, come hundreds of miles, a girl who'd served in the Union Army and was now employed as a spy for a famous detective agency, and she was no better than anybody else.

That thought dismayed her. Almost as much as the nagging doubts she had about Sheldon.

Did he want her out of the house because she was in the way of the job he was doing? Or because he truly was concerned about her?

"I'll be all right," she told him. "You needn't worry for me. I've faced more than Rose Greenhow."

"Evil," he said again, and he leaned his handsome face toward her. "I mean it, Sarah. There is evil in that house. And you should be out of there."

"There's a war on," she said. "There's evil all around us, if you want to use that word. Truly, I'll be fine."

"Just so long as you know you can come to me when things get out of hand," he told her. "Promise me you'll do that. Sarah, forgive me for being so bold, but I think I'm falling in love with you. I know that in normal times and circumstances we wouldn't even have met. But like you said, there's a war on. And everything is topsy-turvy. Everything's changed. What say you to that, Sarah Dawson?"

What could she say? "I like you, too, Sheldon," she told him. She was trembling inside. She could scarce make her voice work right. Happiness flooded through her. But Sarah was too much her father's daughter to believe in such happiness. Hearing Sheldon say he loved her only brought on the new problem of how to banish the differences between their worlds. The world occupied by Rose Greenhow and Mrs. Eugenia Phillips was like Sheldon's, but not hers. It was out of her grasp. She could discuss what was going on in Washington, but she knew instinctively that she was only a spectator and never would be a part of it.

She knew this without question, or without bitterness as to her lot in life. But she knew it with every inch of her bones.

She looked at Sheldon and smiled weakly. "Where would I go if I left? I ran away from home, Sheldon. I never told you that. I can't go back. Not for now at least."

He nodded. "I could help get you another position, if you want it. Remember, my boss is General McClellan. He knows a lot of genteel families in Washington."

"It's good of you to care so, Sheldon."

"I told you why. And I meant it. Can't you say more than that you like me?" He grinned. "Little Rose said I might have a chance with you."

"Oh, Little Rose!" She blushed again. "I do have feelings for you, Sheldon, but we come from such different backgrounds."

"The war is going to change all that."

Sarah shrugged. "Let's get through the war first, and see." She smiled prettily at him. "I think I'll stay where I am for now," she said quietly. "But it's good to know you'll help me if need arises."

"You are quite a girl, Sarah," Sheldon said. "Not like any other girl I've ever met. Ever. And since you are determined to stay, you should know that Rose is going to be visited by lots of important people now that her letter has gotten out. I've been forewarned. And we've got to be ready to receive them."

September 15, Fort Greenhow, Washington

Mrs. Poole was taking the oath of allegiance to the United States in the back parlor.

"Why doesn't she just escape from prison here, like she did in West Virginia?" Rose asked Sarah. "She tied knotted bedsheets together. Surely she could do that here if she wants to get out."

Sarah was getting out Rose's best black bombazine dress, the one with the small net ruffles, so she could receive her visitors. Colonel Thomas Marshall Key, the one administering the oath to Mrs. Poole, was the first to arrive.

At first glimpse of him Sarah had determined that he was elegant and gentlemanly and full of concern for the women prisoners, as well as slightly deaf.

Mrs. Poole had accepted fifty dollars in gold from the United States government, and promised to go on her way and give no more trouble to the United States.

"Fool!" Rose said bitterly, as she sat at her desk in a corner, writing. "It might as well be twenty pieces of silver, as was given to Judas. I knew that woman couldn't hold out. She gave information to Rebel leaders in Kentucky, and now they let her go. Well, they won't get me. I'll not take an oath to any Union! And I'll not wear that dress, Sarah Dawson, so you may as well put it away!"

Sarah had expected this. For her visitors, Rose would not allow any undue fuss, even though Sarah and Medora and Lizzy Fitzgerald all insisted that the house should be thoroughly cleaned and she should wear her best.

"I told you," Rose insisted angrily, "that I'm wearing my oldest calico, and if I had one older I'd wear that. And I want Little Rose in her shabbiest dress and shoes. You tell Lizzy Fitzgerald that if she dresses her up fancy, she'll be put out of this house. This is a prison, Little Rose and I are prisoners, and we'll do it up proudly, thank you!"

Sarah sighed, put away the bombazine gown and reached for the old calico.

Rose put it on. "They are going to try to convince me to sign the oath, too. I just know it. They don't know what to do with me, Sarah. After that letter of mine appeared in the newspapers they dare not hang me, are afraid to release me, and would like to encourage me to escape, in order that they might catch me and spirit me away."

Sarah helped her secure the dress in back. Her figure was still girl-like, she noticed with envy, and she's my mother's age. And even in faded calico she would likely charm her male visitors.

"And they are embarrassed because they hold my child prisoner also," Rose finished. "No, don't fix my hair, Sarah. Leave it. I want to look as disheveled as I can without seeming mad. I must be careful not to act like Mrs. Poole or Mrs. Baxley. These men hold our fates in their hands, dear child. If I act mad, they will put me away."

She took her place in her chair beside her desk and insisted the men be brought up to her. There were two of them now, waiting. She must keep them waiting, she told Sarah.

"Just long enough, but not over long. Like when a woman is courting." She smiled sweetly. "Men are all the same, dear, whether they are sixteen or sixty. They are helpless against a woman's charms. You may tell them they may come up now. I will receive them."

Sarah ran downstairs. In the parlor Captain Sheldon was sitting and chatting with Colonel Key and the Secretary of the Navy, Gustavus Fox, who was fat, bearded, jolly, and extremely embarrassed about his mission.

"I wish to meet this lady who has become so celebrated in the eyes of the world," he said. But Sarah had the feeling that the last thing in the world he was prepared to do was met Rose Greenhow. Rose would eat him for supper, she decided, nothing less.

CHAPTER TWENTY-ONE

September 20, Fort Greenhow, Washington

LITTLE ROSE WAS GOING TO A PARTY. LIZZY Fitzgerald's mother, who lived in the Irish colony of Swampoodle near North Capital Street, was sick. And Lizzy had gone home for two days to tend her.

So the job of caring for Little Rose fell to Sarah. This day she must not only see to the child's wardrobe and hair, but accompany Sergeant Stevens and Little Rose to the home of Mrs. Augusta Morris, near the State Department building.

Rose was begrudgingly allowing Little Rose to go to the birthday party of one of Augusta Morris's little boys. She had told Sarah that Augusta was "full of mean ambition."

"She says she is French. She comes from Virginia. I do not trust her, but Little Rose was once friends with her child and so seldom gets out anymore. I must sew the tear in her pinafore pocket. Come back to my room after you dress her and fetch it. I will not have my child going out into society looking like a vagabond."

It seemed to Sarah that Rose constantly wavered between wanting her child to look like a prisoner and being ashamed of it. She supposed it depended on whom the child was seeing. Or who was observing her. Sarah had long ago noticed that Rose used her daughter for her own ends. And was not ashamed of doing so.

Is this any worse, she wondered, than the way my father used me and Betsy? Oh, I must stop these comparisons. My old life was wrong. And yet there is wrong with the rest of the world, too. I am seeing more and more of it every day.

She and Sergeant Stevens had hired a chaise to take Little Rose to the party in Brown's Hotel, where Augusta Morris was boarding, in style. The weather in Washington had finally cooled, deferring to fall. There would be a crispness in the air. Sarah looked forward to the expedition.

And she had her own mission this day after she helped deliver Little Rose. She had told Sergeant Stevens that she was going to see a dentist, that she had a sore tooth. When indeed, she was slipping out to meet no less than Major Allan himself.

A note had come round in a cake yesterday, crisp and short. But enough to make Sarah's heart rise like the cake itself, light and sweet. She was sure she was being summoned because of the intelligence she'd sent about Rose's tapestry. "Sit down there and I'll run and get your pinafore," she told Little Rose. The child obeyed and Sarah went down the hall to Rose's room.

"Keep an eye on my daughter," Rose said as she bit a piece of thread off in her mouth and handed the crisp white pinafore to Sarah. "Look at the state of that fabric. It's positively threadbare. What my child is suffering because of this war! It breaks my heart!"

Sarah took the pinafore, which she herself had ironed, and started back down the hall. Then, halfway there she held it up to the light. It was scarcely threadbare, she thought. If half the little girls in Michigan had been attired in such a pinafore when they went to school they would have considered themselves wealthy.

But wait, what was this? Something the child had left in the pocket when it was laundered? Funny she hadn't seen it while ironing the garment. She stuck her hand into one of the front pockets and withdrew a piece of paper.

"Tell Aunt Sally that I have some old shoes for the children," the note in Rose's handwriting read. "And I wish her to send someone downtown to take them, and to let me know whether she has found any charitable person to help her to take care of them."

She stood there scowling. The paper was fresh, the ink not running. This note had not run through any process of laundering. And it had not been in the pocket before Sarah gave the pinafore to Rose. She as sure of it!

But what did it mean? This was the note of a spy.

Quickly, she pocketed the note. Obviously it meant something, innocent-sounding as it was. Questions leapfrogged in her mind. Does Little Rose know about this note? Is she to deliver it to somebody in the Morrises' house? Augusta Morris herself, perhaps? Or is Little Rose an innocent pawn, and someone will take it when she is not looking?

Then she remembered. Rose had once told her that Augusta Morris had offered to reveal the signals of the Confederate army to the War Department for ten thousand dollars. Rose had said it was a ruse, to disarm the suspicion that she was a Rebel spy. She had made the remark derisively, pretending contempt for Mrs. Morris. But Rose was in contempt of every other woman in the spy business, was she not?

And maybe that contempt for other women was simply to get detectives off their trail.

Sarah went back into Little Rose's room, tied the pinafore on her, and took her downstairs to find Sergeant Stevens.

"I have only an hour," Sarah told Mr. Pinkerton.

"And you've done more in that hour than most of my other people do in a month," he said. In his hand he had the note Sarah had taken from Little Rose's pinafore pocket. "My God, that woman is bold. I have to admire her, though. And I can only wish she was on my staff."

"But what does the note mean?" Sarah asked. "I thought it was drivel."

"Most of her notes are. What nobody in the War Department could figure out, before they cracked her code, was how such a smart woman could write such trash. What it means is," and Mr. Pinkerton took the stogie out of his mouth to translate, "I have important information to send across the river and wish for a messenger immediately. Do you have any means of getting this information? Please let me know."

"And they've cracked her code?" Sarah asked in disbelief.

"Yes, and thanks to your quick thinking we're going to send a contingent of Sturgis Rifles at noon, while you're away from the party, to get her tapestry. And find out what message is stitched into it."

Sarah took a sip of coffee and a nibble of buttered biscuit and looked around her in the coffee shop of the National, the other hotel on Sixth Street. The marble-fronted Brown's, where she'd left Little Rose under the guardianship of Sergeant Stevens, was in the same block. Both were in the vicinity of the Capital. Negroes lolled outside on the sidewalks, minding the carriages of congressmen who'd come in for the huge breakfast that seemed to last into lunch.

Mr. Pinkerton himself was taking part in that breakfast as he spoke. Fried oysters, steak and onions, blancmange, and paté de foie gras. He suggested Sarah order something. She took only coffee and biscuits. The biscuit stuck in her throat as she conjured up the vision of the crack men from the Sturgis Rifles, likely half a dozen of them, all spit and polish, clomping up the stairs to fetch Rose's tapestry.

In a way she was glad she wouldn't be there.

"You've done good work, Sarah," Pinkerton was saying. "We were wondering how she was getting messages out of the house. Tapestry! Who'd have dreamed it! I must say, it took a woman to take notice of her style."

"Thank you, Sir." Sarah could not help beaming at the praise. She knew it was childish to be so pleased, but she'd waited so long for credit. And coming from Mr. Allan Pinkerton, who demanded so much from his operatives, she knew it was not given lightly.

Then, there she was thinking of home again. And her father. And knowing, in some dim part of her mind, that she'd have stayed home and slopped her father's hogs forever, if he'd only been smart enough to be the one to praise her.

"Do you think Little Rose knows of this note?" Mr. Pinkerton was asking her.

"I don't know, sir. I was going to wait and see if she missed it. If she did, she'll be in a frightful state. The child is dearly afraid of her mother, even though she wants to please her at the same time."

"A feeling not uncommon in children," Mr. Pinkerton said.

Yes, Sarah thought. She knew he was a father and wondered then what kind of a father he was. "I have it planned to tell her that likely she lost the paper in her pocket. And of course, pretend innocence as to what it was. That way I can comfort her and seal our friendship. She likes me a lot."

"Good," he said, "good. If there was a school for spies, Sarah, I'd want you to teach it. Now you had best go. I haven't seen anyone I know yet, and I doubt if any of them could place you, but it isn't good, our being seen together."

"Yes, Sir." Sarah got up. Then remembered. "Oh, Sir, I'm so sorry to hear about Timothy Webster."

"Yes." Pinkerton's face darkened with grief. "I tried to get his coffin sent through the lines but the Rebels refused. They buried him in a pauper's section of Richmond cemetery. After the war I intend to have him disinterred and sent back to Illinois."

"Yes, Sir," Sarah said.

They parted then after Pinkerton told her to be in touch with Kate Warne if anything came up that she felt she couldn't handle.

"And, oh, Sarah," he added, "be careful of Captain Sheldon. We still suspect him of being in sympathy with Rose."

Sarah started out of the hotel, wishing dearly that he hadn't felt it necessary to tell her that. It ruined an otherwise perfect day.

✦ ✦ ✦

When Sarah got back to the suite of Augusta Morris at Brown's Hotel she found Little Rose in tears and Sergeant Stevens unable to console her. The remnants of the children's party were all about, and most of the children had already left. Sergeant Stevens was doing his best, but he was relieved when Sarah appeared.

"How is the tooth?" he asked.

Sarah had forgotten there was supposed to be a bad tooth. Quickly, she told him it was much better, hoping he wouldn't expect her to go into detail because she had never had a bad tooth and didn't know what was expected of one who did.

"The child is inconsolable," he told Sarah. "She said she lost something."

In the background hovered Augusta Morris, small-limbed and dressed in pink. "I told her not to concern herself of the lost note," she told Sarah. "It was only to tell me that she can't eat bananas. But I wasn't serving them. Still, the child is fearful that her mother will know she lost it."

"I'll tell her you received it, then, since you know the contents," Sarah said.

"Oh, you're a dear," Augusta Morris said. Then she laughed nervously. "It was so good to see Rose again. Give my regards to her mother. And tell her the child takes things much too seriously, and she should get out more."

Sarah soothed Little Rose's tears and promised her that she would tell her mother the note was delivered.

"But it wasn't," the child sobbed. "And I can't lie to Mama. She'll know."

"I think your mama has too much on her mind these days. Anyway, Mrs. Morris knew what was in the note. So it didn't matter that it wasn't delivered," Sarah reasoned.

She could say no more in front of Sergeant Stevens. Or, in fact, in front of Little Rose herself. For she was not supposed to know what was in the note. So, with a clear conscience then, she could tell Mrs. Greenhow that, yes, Mrs. Morris did get her message.

And Little Rose was too frightened to deny it.

The child snuggled next to Sarah in the chaise. "I love you, Sarah. I hope you never leave us."

"I hope so, too," Sarah said. And for the moment she meant it. The warmth of the child's slender body in her arms made her feel protective. And loved.

Little Rose gazed up at Sarah. "You'll stay with me always, won't you Sarah? No matter what happens?"

"No matter what," Sarah promised. And she did not, she would not, allow the knowledge of her own lie to ruin the tenderness of the moment.

But then everything was ruined for her again when the chaise pulled up in front of the house on Sixteenth Street to see a contingent of Sturgis Rifles on the sidewalk in front, quickstepping it to march away. All the rifles were held crosswise in front of them. Except for the man in front.

He held Rose Greenhow's tapestry.

As they marched off to the cadence of a captain Sarah did not know, she just stood there and stared. "What happened?" she asked Captain Sheldon. As if she did not know.

"They came for Rose's tapestry. They've taken it. Like they took her books and her husband's papers and her diary. Your work is cut out for you this evening, Sarah," he said. "She's absolutely distraught."

CHAPTER TWENTY-TWO

That Same Night, Fort Greenhow, Washington

ROSE GREENHOW'S SISTER WAS MARRIED TO the nephew of Dolley Madison, wife of the former president. Her niece had been married to Stephen Douglas, who had run against President Lincoln for president. Her son-in-law was with the Union army.

In the bedroom she shared with Rose, Sarah listened patiently that evening as Rose ran down the litany of important people in her family. She did everything she could to make up for the confiscated tapestry. She bathed Rose's forehead with rose water. She ran down to make tea, wishing she had some pennyroyal with butterfly root in it, like she gave Ben at home.

Instead she begged some whiskey from Captain Sheldon, who was more than happy to contribute something. "I can't stand to hear her cry," he said.

And then later he confided to Sarah in the hallway: "I didn't have them come and get the tapestry. I hope she doesn't think it was me. You must tell her, Sarah."

"I will," she promised.

"What else can I do?" he asked.

"Get Little Rose and Medora downstairs for their supper so they don't have to hear this wailing. I'll becalm her."

"You're wonderful, Sarah. I mean it."

Rose's sobs were deep-seated. "It's like I've lost Gertrude all over again. That tapestry was healing to me," the woman mumbled into her pillow on the bed where she'd taken refuge. "It kept me from losing my mind."

Sarah was taken aback at the comparison. Was the woman a complete fool? Or did she just think everybody else was? A piece of tapestry as much a loss as a daughter?

But that would depend, she thought, as she combed out Rose's long, dark curly hair. That would depend on what message was woven into that tapestry, wouldn't it?

The hair-combing quieted Rose, as Sarah knew it

would. Soon the woman slept, still sobbing occasionally, but eventually quieting altogether. Sarah covered her with a light blanket and tiptoed out of the room. Only then did it occur to her that Rose had never even asked her daughter about the message in her pinafore pocket, and if it had gotten to Augusta Morris. And, of course, the child hadn't volunteered any information.

September 23, Fort Greenhow, Washington

It was fully three days later that Sarah learned what was in Rose Greenhow's confiscated tapestry.

On a walk to the confectioner's during her hour off, hoping a message would be awaiting her there, she saw a man hiding in the shadows of the front portal of St. John's Church, a couple of doors up on the other side of the street.

There was no mistaking it. He was signaling to Sarah. Then she recognized Pryce Lewis, the English operative from Pinkerton's. As she crossed the street, he disappeared around the church into the graveyard. Sarah followed.

Under a tree, near a gravestone that said, "Jonas Dupont, Beloved Husband and Father. Fought in Revolution, 1740–1786," they stood alone, talking.

"Major Allan wants you to know," Pryce told her, "the message in the tapestry said that General Ambrose

Burnside will lead a naval expedition from Fortress Monroe to Albemarle Sound, North Carolina, early in January."

Sarah gasped. "All that was in the tapestry?"

"Yes. They have a color code all worked out, she and her superiors. The tapestry was to go to Confederate President Jeff Davis."

"How does she get her information? We know everybody who goes and comes in the house."

"We suspect Colonel Thomas Marshall Key. He came back to the War Department that day after visiting her and begged for her release. He pleaded her cause with Major Allan. Said she is a noble woman and that he wanted to rip the shoulder straps off his uniform after confronting her. Major Allan called his feelings misplaced chivalry and a lack of sternness."

"You mean Key gave her such information?"

"Without meaning to. She has a way with men, Sarah. She gets things out of them, makes them her informants before they realize what they are about. Anyway, Major Allan said he wants you to know how he appreciates what you've done. And keep doing it."

"What else am I to look for?" Sarah asked.

"Anything. If you never find another thing, you've already done enough. But keep at it. And as always, be careful. Toodles."

Then, before Sarah could form the next words in her mind, he gave her a playful salute and disappeared down the walk of the churchyard.

Sarah went on her way to the confectioner's, a rush of happiness flooding through her. The day was pure September, as it should be, as it was in Michigan. The sky was a bowl of Dresden blue, the leaves turning, the sun warm on her face. The elegant brick houses were as perfect as houses could be, with their white shutters, iron railings and fences, and late-summer gardens still in bloom. Someday, she thought, after the war is over I will come back here to Washington and get to know the whole town. Maybe I'll have enough money to rent some rooms in this neighborhood, and then I can stroll on Sixteenth Street and remember back when I was a detective hired out as a maid. And tell my friends about it.

She knew she was having one of those moments that came with a sense of accomplishment, of course. When she felt so complete, so finished, that nobody and nothing could ever make her feel unworthy again.

It won't last, she told herself. It never does. But I'm going to enjoy this moment, this afternoon, just the same.

It didn't last, of course. When Sarah returned to the house after her walk, once again she found a contingent from the Sturgis Rifles. This time they were taking away all Rose Greenhow's paper, all her pens.

They were even taking Little Rose's school supplies. Her mother tutored her every morning, and there were books, paper, pencils, slates. Little Rose had been working on a sampler. They took it away, along with her embroidery threads.

When they took all Rose Greenhow's remaining yarn, Rose was red-faced, confronting them. She held Little Rose close to her. The child was crying. "My daughter is a prisoner! But surely she has a right to an education! You can't take away her school supplies! And her sampler! She was so proud of it!"

"Sorry," the captain of the Sturgis Rifles said, "but we've decoded the message in your tapestry. You've played your last card, Mrs. Greenhow. You should have thought of your daughter's education before you thought of the needs of President Jeff Davis."

"I'm a Southern patriot!" Rose yelled. "I'll not shriek Union to save my skin."

"Then do us a favor," the captain said quietly, "and don't shriek anything. You won't be able to after this, anyway. Orders are you're to be isolated in your room. No more visitors. No more paper, yarn, tapestry. No more teaching your daughter. You brought this about yourself."

"And who is responsible for this?" Rose demanded. "Who ordered that you crack the whip over me this way? Seward? McClellan? Or that German-Jew detective, Pinkerton, whose men are downstairs now going through my things?"

In the hallway Captain Sheldon stood, white of face, watching. Sarah herself was trembling. Rose's voice, whining one moment and indignant the next, grated on her nerves. She was so tired of that voice, she decided. She had such a headache.

What had happened to the beautiful day? To the feeling of completeness she'd felt earlier? Why did it bother her so much that she was responsible for this? She sought Sheldon's eyes, but he would not look at her. Behind Sheldon, Medora lurked, bobbing back and forth like a ghost, and Sarah thought: Nobody ever pays attention to Medora. Have they forgotten she is here? She never complains about anything.

Lizzy Fitzgerald was back, too, standing at the top of the steps. She'd come back just this morning. Her mother had had the typhoid, and died. There was a pall around the usually lively Lizzy. Come to think of it, Sarah thought, there is a pall around this whole house.

Then she looked at Little Rose. The child's eyes resembled the waters of the Potomac after a storm. Muddy, and about to flood over the banks.

Rose had the final word, of course. She always did. "I trust that your next duty, gentlemen, will be a more honorable one than that of guarding helpless women and children," she flung after them as they left.

She is about as helpless, Sarah thought, as a grizzly bear. And yet I feel sorry for her. Oh, I have got to get out of this house. Sheldon is right. There is evil here and it is touching all of us. I must get out soon. I can't stay here now. How can I stay here in the same room with her, when I was the one responsible for all this? How can I sleep next to her and fetch her tea and comb her hair and talk about the small things of everyday life with her?

I have betrayed her as much as she has betrayed the Union. Only I am worse. Because she has not claimed to be a friend of the Union. And I have claimed to be a friend of hers. And Little Rose's.

No, I must leave here soon. I must get word to Mr. Pinkerton. I cannot do this work anymore. I am not corrupt enough for it.

Then everyone was ushered out of Rose's room. Captain Sheldon did his job of closing and locking Rose's door, with her inside. Little Rose was led away crying by

Lizzy, and Sheldon turned to Sarah and said, "I think they mean you not to sleep in there with her anymore. I have orders that she is to be completely isolated until they decide what to do with her." Then it was that Sarah thought, This day can get no worse. No day can.

But it did. That evening. It got much worse indeed.

It was not yet ten o'clock and Sarah was just getting ready for bed in the small room that had once been occupied by Mrs. Eugenia Phillips and her daughters at the end of the hall. Outside her closed door she thought she heard a sound. A cry, from Rose.

She tied her cotton robe tightly around herself, picked up a lighted candle, and opened her door. The way Rose is, she thought, she'd just as soon hang herself to make everyone around her feel guilty. And I can't let that happen. If something is wrong, I must see to it. I am still responsible for watching her, after all.

Sarah heard a noise in Rose's room as she stepped into the darkened hall. What was going on? Rose's door was ajar. It's supposed to be locked, Sarah thought. Who is in there?

She ventured quietly and fearfully down the hall until she could peak in the half-opened door.

There she saw a sight that made her heart fall and crack

open on some terrible place of stone that she never knew she had inside her until this moment, which was like a hardness inside her she knew she never would have discovered back in Michigan. No matter how terrible her family.

Rose Greenhow was in the arms of Captain Sheldon. She herself was in her favorite attire, her ruffled pantalets and chemise, her long hair down her back. His tunic was open in front and they were embracing. She was sobbing into his chest.

"Look what they have done to me. Why do they treat me so, Sheldon? I try to show myself superior to them for the sake of my little girl, but inside I am broken."

"Don't worry," Sheldon was saying, "everything will turn out fine."

"But what will they do to me now?"

"You must be brave," Sheldon told her. "Capitol Prison. That's what I heard. But even if it comes to that, I'll see you are taken care of."

"You will take my note then? And see that it gets to its destination?"

"Yes, I promise."

"Bless you for giving me paper and pen."

"I must take it away now. You understand."

"Yes, certainly."

"You'd best get some sleep now," he advised.

Well, Sheldon, Sarah thought, you are right. There is evil in this house.

She blew out her candle, turned and stumbled back into her room. No wonder Sheldon wanted her out of Rose's room. He wanted her out of the way!

She felt hot, then cold, then she thought she would vomit. Her head pounded as she got into her small bed and drew the covers over her. Oh, Sheldon, she sobbed quietly, how could you?

And then, for the first and last time in her life, she cried herself to sleep over a man.

CHAPTER TWENTY-THREE

September 25, Kate Warne's House, H Street, Washington

SARAH LOOKED AROUND THE TWO ROOMS THAT KATE Warne occupied on H Street and wondered how she could ever have thought them spacious. They were only two rooms, and after the house on Sixteenth Street, they seemed cramped. But Kate was happy here. She remembered, too, envying Kate's independence the first time she'd visited. Kate's bed had been unmade yet, in the middle of the day. And that in itself was a sign of independence to Sarah.

At home an unmade bed in the middle of the day would earn her a cuff from her father. It was a sign of being slovenly and no-count to Isaac Wheelock.

To Sarah, Kate's unmade bed was a sign of the very freedom she was after.

"Your face is flushed," Kate said, as she put the water on the stove for tea. "And you say you've had this headache how long now? Two days?"

"Yes. I wish I had some pennyroyal tea. And other remedies we had at home."

"I can give you a powder for your head," Kate offered.

"I'd like that," Sarah said, "but I'll save it to take tonight when I go to bed."

Why did she have the feeling that Kate was taking her measure, even as she set out the blue cups and saucers, the sugar and cream, and the cake Sarah had brought from her confectioner's?

"So you've got something important to ask me," Kate said.

"Yes." Sarah smiled. "I need your advice. A woman's advice, and you're the only woman friend I have here in Washington."

Kate smiled and sat down at the small table. "You poor

little wretch. That's some assignment you got for your first job. That woman is a handful, so I've been told. I don't know if I could have done the job you did, Sarah."

"Thank you." Coming from Kate, it meant a lot for Sarah to hear that.

Kate poured the tea, and Sarah sat for a while inhaling its fragrance. Then she minded that Kate was waiting for her to speak. "It's about Sheldon," she said.

Kate kept her face straight. "How is the cock of the rock?"

"I caught him the other night in Rose's arms."

Kate near choked on her tea. "You didn't."

"I did." Sarah told of the incident, of what had gone on between them, and the telling seemed to release some of the pain in her head. "Thing is, Kate, I don't know what to do. I know he was just promoted in the Sturgis Rifles. But I saw him take the note from her. And I've seen him take others in the past. Do I tell Major Allan?"

"You've got to," Kate said.

Sarah nodded and bowed her head, hoping Kate wouldn't see the tears in her eyes. "I hope it's the right thing to do, Kate," she said softly.

In a moment Kate knew. She set down her cup and reached her hand across the table to take Sarah's hand. "Don't tell me you're smitten with him, too," she said.

And, when Sarah did not answer, she got up and came around to her side of the table to hug her. Sarah cried then. Washington is the same as home, she thought, while she let the tears roll silently down her face as Kate held her close. As long as nobody gave me sympathy at home, I could take anything. I'd have gone on forever at Rose's house as long as nobody knew my secret and gave me sympathy. But once I get kindness and caring, I'm a helpless heap of nothing.

After a moment Sarah dried her eyes. "Thank you," she said. And to Kate's inquiry of whether she was all right, she assured her, yes.

Kate went back and sat down. "Does he have feelings for you?" she asked.

"He said he loved me," Sarah admitted.

"Do you believe him?"

"After a fashion I do, and after a fashion I don't. I thought he might be saying it just to get my trust, so I'd tell him my real reason for working there."

"Smart girl. You didn't tell him, did you?"

"No. But I'm so confused now, Kate."

"I understand," Kate said. And she said it with such firmness that Sarah knew it to be true.

"But what I don't understand is why you have to ask me about turning him in."

Sarah bit her lower lip until it hurt. "Because I hate him now, Kate, after seeing him in Rose's arms. I hate him for it. And I don't know if I'm going to turn him in because of that or because I should. How am I supposed to know, the way I feel?"

Kate nodded solemnly. "First thing you do," she advised briskly, "is not confide any of this to Major Allan. He'll start to think women can't do the job."

Sarah nodded, agreeing.

"Second, you go to him and tell him what you saw. The facts you saw with your eyes. Let him decide about Sheldon. It isn't your decision to make. But it is your obligation to tell, and leave your personal feelings out of it. Can you do that?"

"Yes," Sarah said.

"Good girl. Whatever happens, happens. But you'll have the consolation of knowing you did your job."

"And what if Sheldon isn't with Rose?" Sarah asked. "What if this is part of some role he's playing?"

"Then you've still done your job. And if he's any kind of a soldier he'll understand it. And respect it, once he finds out what your job is."

"There's just one thing, Kate," Sarah said. "What if he doesn't ever find out? What if I can never tell him?"

Again, Kate Warne looked at her, straight in the eyes.

And in those eyes Sarah saw the answer before she gave voice to the words. "Then you've still done your job, Sarah Wheelock, as you have sworn to do it. And by heaven, in this town, in these times, that ought to count for something."

September 25–26, Back at Fort Greenhow, Washington

Sarah stopped at the confectioner's on the way home, picked up some cake, and sent a message to Mr. Pinkerton, through Iris, about Captain Sheldon.

It occurred to her when she wrote it out that she did not even know Sheldon's first name. His initials were N.E. She had never heard him addressed by anything but Sheldon, and he seemed to prefer it. On the way home she pondered what his first name might be. Neil? Nathan? Maybe it was Newton. She ran all the men's names that began with *N* through her head and decided she liked none of them. But it kept her mind off what she had just done. And off the throbbing of her poor head. And the chills she was feeling.

She put her aches and pains down to nervous exhaustion. Doctor Hammond would know what to do for her. Oh, if only she could see his kindly face. Then, as she neared the house on Sixteenth Street, the sight of which had started lately to fill her with dread, she determined she would ask for a whole day off soon. And get permission to visit Doctor Hammond. Her job here was just about completed. She wondered how Doctor Hammond was doing at his hospital. There had been no more battles since that first one, although there was rumor of battle every day.

Her life in the army seemed like it had been lived by someone else to her now. Her life at home in Michigan seemed like it had happened in the last century.

Sheldon looked pale and near to trembling when she went into the house. "Little Rose is sick," he told Sarah. "I've sent for a doctor."

"What's wrong?"

"Fever and rash. Lizzy Fitzgerald is looking after her. Don't visit her until the doctor determines what's wrong. You know, Lizzy's mother died of typhoid. I'm hoping she didn't bring it into the house."

At the thought of Sheldon's concern for her welfare, Sarah was appalled at the message she had just sent to Pinkerton. She wanted to run from the handsome young captain, but she made herself face him. And she wondered: Was there no end to the bad things that happened in this house?

"Does Mrs. Greenhow need me?" she asked Sheldon.

"No. She's quiet for the moment. We're to avoid her as

much as possible, Sarah. Orders. She is to be isolated, and I'm sorry but that means you, too."

Sarah felt almost an electric field on the floor between them. Sheldon was giving her long, intense looks, and she could not abide it. "I've a headache myself," she told him. "I'm going to my room to lie down. Please knock on my door if Rose needs me."

She took the powder for her head and it relieved the headache in time, but her chills persisted. She wished she was home, for there would be the remedies she needed. If Ben came down with such symptoms, she'd give him a blood tonic, besides the pennyroyal tea. But she had no such herbs here.

With the late afternoon September sun coming in her window she fell into a light sleep. She dreamed of Ben, of her mother. Her sister Clarice was at the kitchen table, sobbing, and then the door of the kitchen opened and her father came in and announced that Clarice's husband was dead, that he had died of wounds received in the Battle of Bull Run.

She awoke with a start, perspiration dripping down her face and neck. Someone was knocking on her door. And, though she was fully awake, someone was still sobbing.

Sheldon stood outside her door. "Rose is carrying on something fierce with the doctor," he said. "She's having high words with him. Little Rose is crying. Can you come?"

She followed him down the hall, the sense of her dreams, the taste of them, the presence of her kinfolk still more real to her than her present surroundings. Just outside the door to Little Rose's room, Sheldon put his hand on her arm, restraining her from entering. In Little Rose's room stood a portly man in an official-looking uniform, with a bushy beard.

"This is Doctor Stewart," Sheldon said. "Doctor, this is Mrs. Greenhow's personal maid and confidante, Sarah Dawson."

The doctor nodded at her. "Perhaps you will be good enough then, Miss Dawson, to tell this lady that I am not going to harm her child."

Rose was standing between him and Little Rose, who lay on the bed, her face flushed with fever. "Perhaps you will be good enough," she told Sarah, "to ask this vulgar, uneducated man, bedizened with enough gold lace for three field marshals, to leave us. He wants to write a prescription for my darling in English, proving he knows no Latin. And on it he misspelled Brigade Surgeon. He writes Brigand-Surgeon. A brigand he is, I'll warrant, but that does not mean I must have him caring for my child."

"Madam," Doctor Stewart said patiently, "I assure you,

I am not uneducated. I have been caring for Mrs. Lincoln herself at the White House."

"Then it is no wonder that lady is constantly in such a state of hysteria," Rose said. "I want my family physician, Doctor McMillan. He is one of the kindest and most chivalrous souls, a gentleman and a man of science. My daughter deserves no less. Sarah, if Sheldon here cannot fill my request, I ask that you do so. Please."

Sarah looked at Sheldon, who nodded yes to her. And she went downstairs to tell Sergeant Stevens at the front door to send immediately for Doctor McMillan.

When she went back inside, Doctor Stewart and Rose Greenhow were arguing.

"Sir, I command you to leave," Rose was yelling.

"Madam, my services have never been refused! Your child has camp measles, and I can treat her malady with expertise."

"Out!" Rose ordered.

"Never have I been so insulted. You are not in possession of your senses, Madam. I shall write a report that you have an aberration of the mind. Your imprisonment has rendered you mad. I shall recommend you to an insane asylum."

He was coming down the stairs, red with rage, as he said this. Immediately Rose threw a book at him in spite of Sheldon's efforts to restrain her. It barely missed his head. The doctor gazed up the staircase at her in amazement, then, as he passed Sarah in the hallway, stopped for a moment.

"The woman is mad," he said. "I must give a full report."

Watching him go out the door Sarah thought, We are all mad. Madness is the normal state of affairs in this house. And, when Sheldon came down the stairs he shook his head sadly. "I'm sorry, Sarah, that you had to witness such. I'm sorry I involved you."

He seemed most sincere, and Sarah's heart ached all the more for it.

Later that evening when Doctor McMillan came, Little Rose cried out so, insisting she would not let him look at her unless Sarah was in the room, that despite Sheldon's objections, Sarah stood beside the child holding her hand the whole time.

Doctor McMillan had the same diagnosis, camp measles. Besides a prescription, he ordered better food, for both Rose and her daughter. More fruit and vegetables. And, when the child was well again, fresh air and exercise.

Sarah waited in the room with Little Rose, holding her hand, giving her water, and telling her stories until the guard came back from Thompson's Drugstore with the prescription. Only when the little girl went back to sleep did she leave, exhausted and careworn, to fall into bed and toss and turn all night in a feverish half-sleep.

In the morning when she awoke, her head was still heavy and aching, and she found that arranging her thoughts was difficult. Alternately, she was hot, then cold. A good breakfast was carried into the house by the guards. Sarah noticed it was much better than the ordinary cold oatmeal mush and tepid coffee. There were coddled eggs, bacon, toast, and a silver urn of hot chocolate.

Sarah looked for Sheldon, realizing what a habit it had become first thing in the morning. When she opened the front door to see his men drilling, Sergeant Stevens was in charge. Casually, she walked into the street. "Where is Sheldon?" she asked him.

"He's been called to the War Department, Miss," Stevens said. "He left me in charge. Said he'd be back in a day or two. Left a message that you should take care of yourself, and stay away from Little Rose until she recovers. And that if you have an emergency, you should have one of us send word to him."

"Thank you." Sarah went back into the house, mounting the steps dizzily. With Sheldon gone she would be expected to be alert and monitor everything that went on in the house. She hoped she could get through the day. She found herself hoping, too, that he would be back sooner than promised. But she knew, inside her bones, that he wouldn't, that he might never be back, and that it was all her fault.

September 28, Fort Greenhow, Washington

It was Saturday, her day off, but Sarah knew there would be no respite for her today with Sheldon away. She had managed to maneuver the last two days without going to pieces, physically or mentally. Now she read in a two-day-old edition of the *Washington Star* that September 26 had been designated by President Lincoln as a day of "humiliation, prayer, and fasting."

Well, Sarah thought grimly, we've done our share of such in this house all along. With Rose Greenhow leading us in the humiliation department.

Her sense of humor was getting black, but she decided it fit the occasion. This day Sheldon was due back. Stevens had told her to expect him before noon.

In spite of Sheldon's orders, she attended to Rose, visiting her in her room, making her bed up, airing out the old linens, and inquiring if she had any needs. It was her job, she decided. She might hate Rose now for what had happened with Sheldon, but it was her job, just like slopping the hogs at home.

The hogs, she decided, betimes had better manners than Rose. But she was determined to put forth her best effort as long as it was demanded of her.

"I'm ill myself," Rose told her. "I feel no sap in me anymore. My child is sick. If I lose Little Rose, I shall die."

Sarah had no sympathy for her, though she did care about Little Rose. But she must maintain a cheerful face, lest Rose suspect her of anything. "You'll not lose her," Sarah promised. Indeed, Rose did not look well. She was pale, there were dark circles under her beautiful eyes, and as she helped her into her dress, Sarah noted there was no more plumpness about her shoulders or arms. Her bones showed, and her skin, usually beautiful, had a sallow cast to it.

Well, Sarah thought, why shouldn't she feel the effects of her imprisonment? The rest of us certainly do. She left the room and went downstairs to await Sheldon. If, indeed, he was coming back. If he hadn't already been placed under arrest. She was nervous and close to frantic, waiting. If he was under arrest, once again she'd be responsible for bringing about a person's dolorous circumstances, and she did not know if she could bear it.

She waited in the parlor, taking up some sewing. To her surprise he came in precisely at ten, to stand in the front door. He came in whistling cheerfully.

Sarah dropped her sewing and stood up. He saw her in the parlor and came in. "Sheldon, is everything all right?" she asked.

He took off his cap, set aside his rifle. "Why shouldn't it be, Sarah?"

"I was worried about you."

"Were you, now."

"Yes."

"Why should you be? You should know by now that I have excellent standing with my superiors, that I am called in every so often to give good account of what's going on here." His face was stoic, giving away nothing. What he did give away she saw in his eyes, the accusation, the sadness. "I'm surprised at you, Sarah," he said. "Don't you know that I have a sterling reputation as someone who has always acquitted himself well? That no matter what untoward thing happens, I always land on my feet?"

Sarah held her chin high, quick in her response. "I didn't know anything untoward had happened," she said.

"Oh? Then why the concern?"

"I always worry when they take you away from us, Sheldon." She tried to walk the line between being discreet and cowering, and found, to her dismay, there was no such line. She was, to her dismay, cowering.

"Actually I was up against some sharp charges," he said in a confidential tone. "As it turned out, someone turned me in, for accepting notes from Rose. Not only that," he gave a short, bitter laugh, "for conspiring with her. The word conspiring is a polite one, it was explained to me, for being discovered embracing her."

Sarah tried to keep from blushing, but found it was something she had no power over.

"Of course, I was detained, while my superiors explained that the charges had to be followed through as a matter of routine. I'm not the only member of the Sturgis Rifles to be charged. Some of my men have been reported as taking bribes from Rose." He glanced at Sarah significantly, then went across the room to gaze out the window.

"Needless to say, all have been cleared. A darned nuisance, all of it. My superiors agree. They even apologized, when it was on report that I did take notes from her and smuggle them out of this house, right to the provost-marshal's office. Notes that helped our cause considerably. As for my being in her arms," he turned, blushing himself somewhat now, "it's part of the job, unpleasant as it is. My superiors know that I did whatever my Presbyterian conscience permitted to secure information from her in order to pass it on. It's just too bad that whoever saw us in that compromising situation did not understand it, too."

Relief flooded Sarah. She could feel it going from her head to her toes, draining her. And she could not help but admire his confidence, his bearing. It showed years of proper upbringing. He is truly from quality people, she decided. Oh, I am so glad he is innocent!

"Oh, Sheldon, I am happy for you." And she started toward him. But he held himself rigid, military-style, and walked right by her to the hall, picking up his rifle and hat as he did so.

"Are you, Sarah? Why? Because my name is cleared? Or because when you saw me in Rose's arms the other night, I was only doing my job?"

"Sheldon, what are you saying?"

"I don't think it has to be spelled out, Sarah, do you?" He smiled at her, but in the old heart-tearing, endearing smile she found only icy dismissal now. "Not even to you. I asked you for your trust. If you'd given it, if you'd told me what you were about here we could have worked together. Instead you chose to suspect me. I'm hurt beyond belief, Sarah. And being in charge here I think it is truly time you left this house."

It was worse than a slap for Sarah, hearing him say such. Worse than any blow she'd received from her father.

Worse than being made to kneel beside the table while he ate, for not doing her chores right. And the blow made her physically reel. She felt the floor tilt beneath her. No, the whole world was tilting. And she ran from the room, even while the walls were closing in. Because, no matter what, she did not want to faint at Sheldon's feet.

CHAPTER TWENTY-FOUR

September 30, Kate Warne's House, H Street, Washington

SARAH DREAMED. HER DREAMS MADE NO SENSE AND honored no rhyme or reason, but the very strong presence of certain people in them rendered them real.

In the landscape she traveled, certain places were familiar, because she'd traveled them before in dreams. One scene was a ridge that overlooked a river. It had precarious drops into the water below, and wound along paths she'd taken before, always with the terror of being lost, with her destination never to be found. In this dream she had her brother, Ben, with her and he was sickly and she had to get him to town to a doctor. Ben's presence dominated the dream.

In another dream she was in Flint, Michigan, trying to find Aunt Annie, but the streets had no resemblance to the Flint she knew. Yet every time she dreamed it, the streets were the same, with twists and turns that confused her. In this dream the presence was Betsy, her sister. She was trying so hard to bring Betsy to Aunt Annie's, to get her out from under her father's rule. But she and Betsy always ended up lost.

Usually when she woke up the scenery would be difficult to recall, but the closeness of either Betsy or Ben lingered with Sarah. But this morning when she woke, she was in terror.

"I've got to get Ben to the doctor," she yelled. "He's got typhoid!"

"Ssh, Sarah, ssh." The voice was familiar. She opened her eyes and tried to clear her vision, but it was as if she were underwater, looking up. "Where am I?"

"You're with me." It was Kate Warne's voice. "You've been ill, Sarah. Very ill. Your fever finally broke."

Her nightdress was damp and as she struggled to sit up and see, Kate helped her. Kate's voice pulled her out of the swampy miasma that threatened to envelope her so completely.

Sarah looked around. She was indeed in Kate's place, in her very bed as a matter of fact, weak and with her short curly hair plastered in perspiration around her head. "What happened to me? How did I get here?"

"You fainted two days ago at Rose's house. Sheldon sent word to his superiors and they sent you in a chaise to me."

"Two days ago? I've been here two days?"

"Yes. Doctor Hammond was here. Major Allan sent for him."

"Doctor Hammond? He cared for me?"

Kate grinned. "You were out of your head, Sarah. You called him Sheldon and struck out at him. He ordered quinine for you. And other prescriptions. You slept like a babe for two days."

Sarah sank back on the pillows. "Why didn't you wake me so I could talk to Doctor Hammond? And Major Allan?"

"You were either dead to the world or delirious."

"Oh, I'm so embarrassed. What do I have?"

"Doctor Hammond said you had a type of malignant fever. He calls it Potomac fever. He'll be coming again to see you and explain. Sheldon told me that Lizzy Fitzpatrick's mother just died of typhoid. Is that true?"

"Yes. What else did Sheldon tell you?"

"He was just worried about you, Sarah. He was very professional and soldierly. What else did you wish to hear?"

"Nothing," Sarah said. Professional and soldierly, she thought. But not professional enough to understand. I was only doing my job. She closed her eyes. "I think I just want to sleep."

October 4, Kate Warne's House, H Street, Washington

The next time Doctor Hammond came Sarah was sitting on the settee in Kate's parlor, which was really part of the kitchen. She was freshly groomed, thanks to Kate, and wearing one of her friend's silken robes.

She was so glad to see her old friend, she started to cry. "Oh, Doctor Hammond, I thought I'd never see you again."

He sat down next to her, "You'll have more trouble than that getting shut of me, Sarah Wheelock. I've kept track of you, you know. Checked in regularly with Mr. Pinkerton."

Sarah was touched. No one had ever cared to keep track of her doings. She felt the warmth of his concern, the pleasure of being looked after.

"Kate tells me your fever has broken."

"Yes, Sir."

He took her hand, feeling her pulse. "You're a lucky girl. Thanks to your caring friends who got me in time. I've got some new vaccine from the Surgeon General's office that's going to be given out to all the hospitals starting tomorrow."

"I thought the dose of bitters you made us all take back at the hospital would have protected me from such sickness."

He laughed. "Likely it protected you from getting the typhoid. I believe that Lizzy Fitzgerald brought it back from her mother's."

"But she wasn't sick," Sarah told him.

"Some people are carriers. I firmly believe that, though I can't prove it. There are many kinds of fever in Washington these days, Sarah. Typhoid, malaria, remittent and bilious. All the hospitals are full of men with fever."

"So you've been busy," Sarah said.

"Yes, and not only with that. I've been helping the medical director of the Army of the Potomac. We've been formulating plans for frame buildings to accommodate at least fifteen thousand men. We can no longer rely on hotels, schoolhouses, churches, and public buildings."

"And you've come here to see me. I feel guilty keeping you from your work," Sarah said.

"You'll only feel guilty if you don't let me vaccinate you," he answered. "And you, too, Mrs. Warne. I'm grateful to you for caring for Sarah. But you must take precautions yourself."

He vaccinated them both. Kate was braver than Sarah, but Doctor Hammond said she'd been brave enough in the past for any two women he knew. The vaccination involved some scratching on the arm where the vaccine went in. Then he advised more rest and good food for Sarah, and left.

The next day while Sarah was sleeping, Nubbin came around and delivered a cooked chicken and some fresh fruit and bread. Sarah was devastated that she had missed Nubbin, and she cried for missing him. She cried at the drop of a handkerchief, it seemed. And back home she'd never cried. What was wrong with her?

Kate said she had a slight fever again from the vaccination, and put it down to that. Sarah berated herself for that, then. "Why didn't you get a fever?" she asked her friend. "Why am I suddenly such a sissy-boots?"

"You have been through a crisis of the soul as well as the body," Kate said. "You must be patient with yourself. And allow yourself to heal."

All this talk about a crisis was new to Sarah, especially out of the mouth of a strong, widow-woman like Kate. Such tenderness and acknowledgment of her troubles as real was new to her, too. At home there had been no time or energy devoted to caring about the state of the souls of the women in the household. Much less their bodies.

Kate said she had a week between assignments, so she stayed home and cared for Sarah that first week. Never had Sarah been so exhausted in her life! As the trees outside Kate's apartment windows turned red and gold in the October sunlight, she took her ease, reading and resting, thinking of Sheldon, going over in her mind the conversations between them, remembering his smile, wondering what she would do differently if she had the chance, and crying when Kate wasn't about.

The second week she was stronger. Kate went back to work and Sarah spent time straightening the place, even doing some cooking. Kate was on another assignment, but came home nights.

Kate never mentioned Sheldon. Neither did Sarah. But she did not have to, for he was there always, in her soul, part of her, more than she had allowed to herself that he was. She found suddenly how much he was part of her. She measured everything in life by the pleasure and the pain of knowing him. She had, unwittingly, done what she vowed she would never do as a woman. She had allowed the idea of a man, the remembrance of him, to seep into her bloodstream and change the very fiber of her being.

The war was not anywhere near Washington now. Sarah read in the papers about President Lincoln calling for a movement into east Tennessee, there was a brief skirmish at Springfield Station, Virginia, and the Confederate government made a peace treaty with the Great Osage Indian tribe. But everyone was still waiting for the next big action.

October 20, Kate Warne's House, Washington

Then, toward the end of October Kate came home and told her that she'd heard that Rose Greenhow was being sent to Old Capitol Prison.

Sarah's first thought, now that she was getting stronger, was for Little Rose. "Is the child going to that terrible place with her?" she asked Kate.

"Yes. You know Rose by now, Sarah. Major Allan says she wouldn't think of going without her. The child brings her sympathy. Little Rose heightens her plight with the public."

"I've heard there are terrible people in that place, not to mention vermin and disease," Sarah said. "How can she take Little Rose with her?"

"It's her choice," Kate reminded her.

"Do you think there's a chance I can go along? Shall I ask Major Allan?"

"To what end?" Kate asked. "When Rose likely knows by now who you are?"

Sarah contemplated that, thinking. "And has told Little Rose. Oh, Kate, I can't bear having the child think I betrayed her! She looked to me so! I promised I would always be around as a friend for her!"

"That's the hardest part of this job, Sarah. I wanted to tell you before, but we all have to find it out for ourselves. We tend to become fond of those we are supposed to be reporting on. I don't know of any other case Major Allan has taken on that involved children. Yours was likely the first. And he knew you would be good, because you are his youngest agent and could get close to the child. Oh, Sarah, don't cry!" Kate sat next to her on the settee. "Think of the wonderful job you did for your country. If you hadn't made friends with Little Rose, you wouldn't have found the diary! And so many of those arrested would still be doing their mischief, including the mayor of Washington, who was in the plot to detach Maryland from the Union!"

Sarah wiped tears from her face with the back of her hand. "You're right, of course. But still, I'd like to see Little

Rose. Even from a distance. Do you think I could? When do they go to prison, Kate?"

"This afternoon." Kate looked worried. "I suppose I could get you across the street near St. John's. It's a favorite place of all of us to watch the doings at Rose's. But we cannot be seen."

Sarah promised. And then it came to her. Likely, she'd see Sheldon, too. Oh, she thought, Sheldon.

In the portal of St. John's Church, which gave good protection, they waited in the shadows. The October afternoon was warm, and dozens of people were already congregating outside Rose's house, held off physically by the Sturgis Rifles. They were waiting to see Rose taken to prison. Grown men, women of quality, even little children were gathered in the street and across it, to watch the spectacle.

"I'm ashamed of myself," Sarah told Kate. "But I'm not here for the same reason as these others, to ogle. Still, I'm ashamed."

"You want to stay? Or leave?" Kate asked.

"I'd like to stay and see Little Rose. If she's perky and looking well, I'll feel a lot better about things."

Kate took her arm. "Then let's go to the back of that crowd over there. No fear we'll be seen."

They took their places carefully, trying to blend in as best they could. They did not have long to wait. In about ten minutes the carriage came and the men of the Sturgis Rifles herded the crowd back. Sarah saw Sergeant Stevens, but he was concentrating so on his task at hand that he did not notice her, for which she was glad.

Out of the carriage stepped Mr. Pinkerton. With him were Pryce Lewis and another man. "John Scully," Kate murmured. Immediately they went into the house, and for what seemed like an endless amount of time, the crowd waited.

"How did these people know?" Sarah asked Kate in amazement.

"Likely Rose had word smuggled out that she was being moved."

"Then she's still getting out messages."

"And she will. Even in prison. I guarantee it," Kate said, then fell silent. The front door of the Sixteenth Street house opened and a collective gasp went up from the crowd as Mr. Pinkerton came out leading Rose, who was holding on to her daughter. The two other Pinkerton men followed.

For one brief moment Rose stood there on the top step, dressed in her best, Sarah noticed. And waved to the crowd. At once a cheer went up in the street. And she blew kisses.

"Rose, Rose, Rose," the crowd chanted, louder and louder. Sarah saw the men from the Sturgis Rifles hold their guns up in front of them to hold the crowd back. There were many more men than had been at the house before. At least fifty of them now, all solemn and ready to perform their task. Rose waved and held up her hand for silence. The crowd hushed.

"Abraham Lincoln has written in words of blood," she called out, "upon the tablets of history, that the Great Model Republic is a failure."

The people cheered, then went silent again, waiting for more. Why, Sarah thought, they are all secessionists! They are all betrayers of the Union!

It was frightening to her that all these people could gather in the middle of the day in the nation's capital and proclaim their hatred of the Union. It was more frightening to hear such sentiments so boldly spoken by Rose.

What have I been thinking? Sarah wondered. I have truly had a crisis of the soul, as Kate called it. Of course, I have done the right thing here! How can I ever have thought otherwise?

Kate was looking down at her, her blue eyes twinkling, as if to say, "You see?"

Sarah smiled at her. "Let's go," she said. "I've seen enough."

"But there is Little Rose," Kate whispered. "Don't you want to see her? Look, she's dressed in all her finery."

"No," Sarah said.

"And look, there's Sheldon. Look, Little Rose is hugging him."

This time Sarah looked, but could not see for the tears in her eyes. Well, Sheldon would hug Little Rose. For that she wouldn't blame him. But he could have made some allowances for what she was doing, she thought. He could have understood, couldn't he? After all, we are both on the same side. He could have forgiven me. After all, what I had to suffer as part of my job, he had to suffer too, didn't he?

Only I *can't* fix loving Little Rose. And he *can* fix being angry at me. Only he won't. So it has nothing to do with our jobs then, does it? And maybe it never did.

"Come on, Kate," she said, "I've really seen enough. Let's go."

CHAPTER TWENTY-FIVE

November 4, North of Flint, Michigan

SARAH GOT OFF THE RIVERBOAT IN HER LITTLE town of Casey's Mill, Michigan, without being recognized in her boy's clothing. Though the sun was shining, Casey's Mill, like Sarah, seemed to have the dismals.

Or was it just that it did not have the bustle of Washington City?

A few other passengers disembarked with Sarah. And some others were getting on. She recognized no one. Teams of hardy horses attached to work wagons waited at the edge of the levee for anyone who needed a ride. They would belong to Mr. Blendheim. He never let a riverboat passenger be stranded without a ride. On the platform she saw large containers of milk being shipped off to a creamery downriver. Likely, some of them were from her father's farm. And she knew just which ones they were. The more battered ones. The sight of them gave her a pang. Nothing had changed here, after all. Then, looking around, she decided something had.

There was a corral with a number of horses inside adjacent to the levee. People were shipping horses on the riverboat. Sarah wondered if they were for the army. Then she spied the carpetbags of a traveling salesman and somebody's trunk. Before, Sarah never would have taken note of such things. But now that she was a trained detective, she had an eye for detail.

She snuggled inside the warm coat with the beaver collar that she'd managed to wrangle from one of Pinkerton's agents who was spending the winter in the South. She'd return the coat, and boots she wore, as well as the woolen trousers and leather gloves. Because she was going back to Washington after she visited home. Mr. Pinkerton had asked her to come back and work for him. Doctor Hammond had said if she didn't want to do that, he could find her a place with Dorothea Dix. Or Clara Barton, the famous woman who was organizing Washington's field hospitals and a nurse corps.

Sarah was determined to go back after this trip. She'd already made up her mind. She was going back to work for Mr. Pinkerton.

But she had something to do first. She had to go home.

Both Mr. Pinkerton and Doctor Hammond had insisted she take the trip to rest, and get away from the war for a while. Sarah had told them she was going home, but she hadn't divulged that it was as a boy. Only Kate knew that. Kate had understood. Sarah was still afraid that somehow, her family would try to stop her from leaving once she got home. Or that their need for her would be so dire that she would feel compelled to stay.

This way, if she came as a stranger, just passing through, they would not know who she was. She had fooled the army, hadn't she? Certainly she could fool her family.

The dock agent was busy seeing to the loading of farm goods and baggage. Thank heavens, Sarah thought. He knows me. Mr. Knapp was his name. How many times he had held the boat, waiting for Sarah and Betsy to arrive in their wagon with the milk cans. He was a good man.

She made her way through the usual assortment of people who came to the docks because they had nothing better to do. And there was a young Ira Cooperman, pencil and pad in hand, making note of the arrivals for the town's small paper, the *Daily Bugle*.

Sarah went down the platform steps before he could ask who she was. Should she rent a horse? Or ride in one of Mr. Blendheim's wagons?

A horse would lend itself better to her plans, she decided. That way she could wander the countryside as she pleased, and get a good look at everything again. And she could leave her father's place in the middle of the night if she did not like the way things were going.

Behind her as she made her way across the street she heard the tooting of the riverboat whistle. The pilot sometimes did that for children who came to the docks. Sarah noticed that they weren't loading the horses and wondered why.

Kettle's Livery was just the same as always. In no time at all she had rented a horse, paid Mr. Kettle's assistant, and was off down the familiar roads and paths and lanes of her childhood.

At first she just went in a plodding walk. The horse was middling, not at all like Sarah's Max. She wondered what had happened to Max, but then didn't have to ponder long. Her father, never willing to give up anything that was his, would have sent for him, or gone to Flint to fetch him home himself, once he discovered Sarah was gone. Likely he'd count the horse's worth as more than hers. She laughed to herself. Such things no longer bothered her.

She increased the horse's gait from a plodding walk to a half-trot as the afternoon waned and the November sun sank behind the trees. Nights were cold here. Much as she wanted to drink in the familiar sights, she wanted to get to the farm just after dusk, she had to hurry.

The Wheelock farm was halfway down the slope of a mountain ridge, on a plateau of good rich land the ice had formed tens of thousands of years ago when it came down from the top of the world. That's what Mr. Roane, Sarah's teacher in the one-room school she'd attended, had told them. He'd made them learn all about the Ice Age, and how Michigan once sat in the line of the overhang of that ice and how, at night in winter, if you listened hard, you could hear the wind blowing down from the great dark north, contriving to make another Ice Age that would cover them all.

From where she sat on her horse, in a line of timbers on the mountain ridge, she could see their farm like God might see it. All the carefully tended fields, now fallow in the November dusk, the barn, the small creek over which

Ezekiel Kunkle had come that day, the lines of fencing that held in the cows, and the house, snug and nestled in contentment, with the smoke curling out of its chimneys.

Lights glowed from within. There was a thick frosting of snow on the ground, in patches here and there. Crows cried across the remnants of old corn husks in the fields. The lights came from the kitchen. The family would be at supper. In the distance, carried on the cold November air, she heard the distant barking of Mose.

As if nothing happened since I left, Sarah thought. As if there had been no Battle of Bull Run, no recruiting sergeant in Flint, no Doctor Hammond needing food or Nubbin waiting to fetch it in his wagon, no suffering patients in the tent hospitals or men dying after battle in the rain. No woman in the middle of the road who had refused to move because she claimed she was cooking her husband's supper.

As if she hadn't slept between two dead men, or seen a man's heart beating through his torn-open chest because she'd shot him. As if there had been no Mrs. Briscoe to shoot at her, then turn her in as a woman. No Mr. Pinkerton saying he needed her. No Kate Warne or Rose Greenhow or Little Rose.

As if she'd never given her heart to a Lieutenant

Sheldon, or turned in information to the War Department about a woman sending messages in her tapestry that could result in the deaths of thousands.

The farm was the same. All the same. Untouched by the horror, betrayal, and fear of the war. Only she had changed. So much so that she'd have been surprised if Mose didn't bite her. And she pressed her knees to the horse's sides and went down the slope to the fertile plateau that had been formed by the indifferent ice tens of thousands of years ago.

A quick step inside as she knocked on the door. Mose, tied up near the barn, was barking as if the whole Rebel army was encircling the house, and the other hounds her father kept took up the chorus.

"Yes?" Her mother's voice. She tried to keep her heart from racing.

"Got lost on the road, Ma'am. And my horse needs some food and rest." She used her man's voice, her army voice. Her family had opened its house dozens of times in the past to such a request. Everyone in these parts did. The door opened, and her mother stood there, holding a lantern. Behind her was the familiar kitchen scene, table laid for supper, her brother Ben in the chair by the hearth working on making something out of wood, her sister Betsy by the hearth, tending to a pan of muffins.

Why hadn't her father come to the door as he always insisted on doing? The question pushed from the back of her mind, but then the sight of her mother's familiar, worn face pushed it back.

"Name's Neddy Compton," she said. "I'm on leave from the Army of the Potomac. On my way over to Hillsdale, just over the next mountain. Only I think my horse went a little lame, and I'm asking for a bite. For me. And some hay for the horse, and to maybe bed in the barn for the night."

She knew her mother had long since lost contact with any friends in Hillsdale since Mrs. Harris had died.

For a moment her mother's blue eyes showed concern. Then they brightened. "On leave, you say? Where did you serve, Mr. Compton?"

"Washington. Battle of Bull Run."

"Oh, do come in. My son-in-law served in that battle. He was killed. We just received word at the end of October."

Oh, no, Sarah thought, as she stepped over the threshold and the warmth and smells of the house enveloped her, Clarice's husband, dead.

"I'm sorry for your loss, Ma'am," she said.

"Take off your coat," her mother insisted. "Do sit down.

We're just two women in this house now, and my son, Ben, who is not fit for the army, though he did recently try to enlist."

Ben got up from his chair by the hearth and came across the room to take Sarah's hand. His eyes swept her face, and Sarah felt his warm grip. "Army wouldn't have you?" she asked.

"Not even the Quartermaster Department," Ben said. "Especially when they learned Pa died just August last. Killed in a hunting accident. Fell down a ravine. And my sister who did most of the work around here lit off."

That must be the ravine on the other side of the creek, Sarah thought. On Ezekiel Kunkle's property. Pa often hunted there. But he knew the ground.

Ben seemed taller. He seemed to be standing a little straighter. He had good color in his face, as if he'd been outdoors a lot.

Sarah took a seat where her mother directed. "Glad to have the company," her mother said. It was her father's place at the table. Sarah felt strange sitting in his chair. She was struck by the fact that he was gone. August, Ben had said. What had she been doing in August? Caring for whining Rose Greenhow, whose oldest calico dress was newer than her mother's best one.

There were muffins and potato soup for supper. Sarah

marveled at the tastiness of the soup, then recollected how her mother could make the plainest fare palatable. Betsy sat across from her, jumping up every so often to check something cooking on the hearth. There was a piece of meat frying. Sarah's mouth watered. And the house enveloped her, put its arms around her, remembering her. And yet, at the same time, closing in. The ceiling too low, the walls too thick, the whole place constraining her, choking her, like she'd seen Rose choked by the corset she wore under her gowns to diminish her waistline.

Sarah had vowed never to wear a corset like that. Never.

So, in order to keep herself from being pulled into the old memories, the feelings, and the need she already sensed here for her presence, she thought of the house as a corset, which would choke her and take the breath right out of her if she stayed.

"Did your son-in-law live here?" she asked. She was careful to keep her voice deep, as she'd done in the army. She was grateful she'd had the mole on her face removed. They did not recognize her.

"Not far," her mother said. "And, of course, his wife and child are alone now. We expect Clarice will be moving back in with us."

"A terrible thing, this war," Sarah said.

"Were you wounded in the battle?" her mother asked.

"No, Ma'am."

"Then you wouldn't have had occasion to be near any hospital."

"Oh, I wouldn't say that, Ma'am. I had Potomac fever. Why?"

"Did you come across any woman nurses? I lost a daughter, you see." Her mother's voice broke and then she quickly recovered herself. "I think she ran away to Washington to become a nurse. She was visiting with my sister in Flint when she went missing. She was most acquainted with remedies and herbs, and knew about the art of healing. Her name was, is Sarah Louisa. She is very pretty. She had a mole on her cheek."

"In the time I was in the hospital, Ma'am, I was feverish and out of my head. I can't say," Sarah told her. All the while she kept her head lowered. Ben was looking at her in a most quizzical way.

They talked about the war the rest of supper. The family was starved for news. Sarah told them all she knew, feeling most wordly.

"I thought you were come to buy horses," her mother said then. "Army men come through this part of the country regular-like. They've bought up a lot of the good stock and are always looking for more. My son, Ben, here has taken the riverboat once or twice with the shipment of horses to keep them safe. He's even gone on the train with them, far as Baltimore."

"I know the army needs horses," Sarah said. "That must be some trip, Ben. I saw some horses in the corral adjacent to the docks."

"They're awaiting shipment tomorrow," Ben said. "Yes, it's a trip, all right. It takes me away from here about two weeks. But the pay is good, and I get to see some of the world. I make the trip with Harmon Johnston's son from over to Hillsdale. Josh. He's only sixteen and wants to join the army. His pa lets him make the run on the promise he won't join up until he's eighteen."

So the war had come to this area, Sarah thought. Then finally, unable to contain herself any longer, she asked, "Do you all bring the harvest in yourselves, after you lost your husband, Ma'am?"

"We had help," her mother said. "A neighbor. A Mr. Kunkle. He's been more than helpful. We couldn't have done it without him."

"He's a good man," Betsy chimed in. "A widower, with small children. Of course, Ma minded the children while he and I, and even Ben here, brought in the harvest."

Something there was in Betsy's eyes. Some newfound

maturity that Sarah recognized, some roundness in her face that bespoke contentment and satisfaction.

Sarah nodded, and knew. With a sense of alarm and outrage, she knew, so that when Betsy finally spoke the words they were unnecessary.

"We've become betrothed," she said happily.

Well, so Betsy had found a man to take over the farm-work. She had always thought her sister would elope with the first man who asked. But Ezekiel Kunkle?

"I'm happy for you," she said. "He must be a good man."

"Not only that," Betsy said, "but our two farms will merge. He has a beautiful spread across the creek. You likely passed it on your way."

Sarah put down her spoon, struck with the thought of how much of an accident her father's death had really been in that ravine on Ezekiel Kunkle's property. Had Kunkle shot her father? Then she looked into Betsy's face as her sister poured more coffee into her cup and saw the smile in Betsy's eyes. No, she decided. It must have been an accident. Not even Betsy could wed a man who'd shot her own father. And Betsy would know, because sooner or later, in one of his boastful moments, Kunkle would have told her.

Ben was still watching her from the other end of the table. But then there was another problem. What would become of Ben once Ezekiel took over? Because that's what

Kunkle was after, even if her father's death was an accident: their farm. And someone to take care of his children.

Where would Ben fit in? What would happen to him? He didn't fit in at all, Sarah knew. So then, what was she supposed to do about it?

She was tired from her train trip, which had taken most of the day, from the fifteen-mile ride from town, and the onslaught of emotions that came with going back inside her own house and sitting at the table with her own people, and keeping up the pretense of being someone else. Just the sights and the smells of home wore her out.

"I thank you for the supper, Ma'am," she said to her mother. "But I'm pure worn down. I think I'll bed in the barn and see to my horse if you don't mind. And I'll be off in the morning."

"Oh." Her mother looked up as she stood. "Won't you have some apple cake? Betsy's apple cake in the best in the county. She won first place for it at the fair in the fall."

"Did she?" Sarah asked. "Well then, if you don't mind I'll take some to the barn with me."

Betsy jumped up, anxious to show her talents, and cut a piece of the cake, then carefully wrapped it in a napkin, and handed it to her. "I get up early, me and Ben," she said, "to milk the cows. We'd be glad to give you hot coffee and muffins before you start on your way."

"Thank you," Sarah said. Then she turned, her head swimming, picked up her coat and put it on, and took the lantern that Betsy handed her.

"We can put you up in my daughter Sarah's room if you like," her mother offered.

"No, thank you, Ma'am," Sarah answered, "The barn will be fine."

Her own room was too much to ask. She knew she did not have the mettle to withstand the pull of home if she slept in her own bed. She knew, too, that she must get away from here before her feelings enveloped her completely. Before she went to her mother and threw her arms around those thin shoulders in the shabby dress and said, "It's me, Ma. It's your very own Sarah. Don't let Betsy marry that evil man or soon he'll be knocking her about just like Pa treated you. And soon she won't be so confident or pretty anymore. Don't let him take the farm, Ma. What will he do to Ben? Don't let him have it."

But if she did that, she'd have to stay. She'd have to incur Betsy's wrath, then who would help her run the place? She couldn't do it on her own, and Betsy might wed herself to Kunkle anyway and he'd come and live here in spite of her. And make her one of his field hands. And she could do nothing about it.

Her mother may have already signed the place over to

him for all she knew. Her mother had no sand in her when it came to allowing men to tell her what to do. And from the look in Ben's eyes, this was already true.

She started out the door. The quicker she got out of there the better for everybody. And then Ben reached out his hand. "I'll show you to the barn, Mr. Compton," he said. "It's the least I can do."

It was Mose who gave her away. Mose knew her right off as she approached the barn. He was tied up, but he jumped on his hind legs and whined and yelped, and Ben said, "Never saw anything like it, how that dog takes to you, Mr. Compton."

Then Ben did a strange thing, a thing Sarah knew he never would do if he didn't believe in his own instincts. He untied Mose, who would bite off a stranger's leg if he didn't take to him.

Mose ran right over to Sarah, leaping with joy, jumping up to lick her face. She embraced him, patted him, of course. "Good dog," she said, "good dog."

Then they went into the barn, the three of them, and Ben set the lantern down. "That looks like one of Mr. Kettle's horses," he said.

"Yes," Sarah agreed. "I rented it."

There was a whinnying from one of the stalls. And it

tore at Sarah's heart. It was Max, who also recognized her. She turned to see his large liquid eyes, his soft velvety nose bobbing up and down over the stall gate.

Ben was watching her closely. She knew if she went to Max now, all would be over for her. She also knew that Ben wanted her to, was waiting for her to.

She looked at her brother, tears in her eyes. "He's waiting for you," Ben said. "Ezekiel Kunkle wants him for his own, you know. I begged Ma not to give him, but she did. She's given everything to that man, signed it right over. It's his and Betsy's now."

Sarah went swiftly to Max's stall, embraced her horse, who nuzzled her, whinnying a soft welcome. "How did you know?" she asked Ben without looking at him.

"Well, hell's bells, Sarah, I held to the fact all the time that you ran off to join the army. Ma said no, you never would. She said the nursing corps. Well, which was it?"

"The army," Sarah said. "You were right. I made it through Bull Run before I got caught out. Then they offered me a job in Pinkerton's detective service. I took it. And I'm going back, Ben. They want me back," she said.

Still holding on to Max's neck, she faced Ben determinedly.

"What happened to the mole?" he asked. "That was the

only thing that put me off. I was in doubt, until Mose and Max here proved me wrong."

"I had it removed in the army, lest anybody from home in the 2nd Michigan see me and recognize me."

"No reason why you shouldn't go back," he said. "There's nothing for you here. You know what this place will become once Kunkle takes over. And they wed before Christmas."

Sarah nodded. "What will happen to you, Ben?" she asked.

"I'll find my way. I always have, haven't I? They've offered me a job, teaching at our old school." He grinned. "Can you see me as a schoolmaster?"

"I think you'd be good at it, Ben."

"They'd give me lodging at the school. You know, like they did for Mr. Roane. He went off to the army, Sarah. They've got Miss Byron teaching now, but nobody likes her. It might be good to get away from here, but I don't know. Some of those boys are so big and rough and they might not respect me if I couldn't take them in hand when I had to. Course, if I went, I'd take Mose with me. Wouldn't leave him here with Kunkle."

They stood in silence for a while, Sarah petting Max and looking around the familiar barn to everything she remembered so well. All the while, Sarah was thinking.

"Ben, I'm leaving in the morning, you know. Like I said. I'll kill Kunkle if I stay here. I'll not be able to bear what becomes of Betsy."

He nodded. "I kind of hoped you'd tell Mama," he said.

"I can't, Ben," she said. "I can go up against anything, the house, the animals, what I know will happen to Betsy, anything. But not Mama's asking me to stay. I'd rather go up against a whole Rebel battery than that."

Ben smiled. "So what do we do, then?"

"You can tell her after I leave. Only so she knows I'm still alive and well. It'll take the burden from her. But, since I'm not of age yet, you can't let Betsy or Kunkle know. He'll be head of the family, and he could get me sent back. You will do that for me, Ben, won't you?"

"Yes," he said.

"And I'll do something for you," Sarah said. She left Max and went to stand in front of her brother. "I'll give you an address in Washington where you can reach me anytime it gets too bad here for you. I know enough people there now that I could likely find you a position, Ben. Even with Mr. Pinkerton. You don't have to be —" She stopped and began again. "Your problem wouldn't prohibit you from working for Mr. Pinkerton."

"Thank you, Sarah, but likely I'll stay around here for a

little while, even if it means taking the teaching job, just to make sure everything is all right with Ma."

In the morning, early, Ben woke her, as they had agreed. It was still dark in the barn and Sarah hated to get out from under the heavy quilts Ben had given her, but he had hot coffee and bread and cheese for her, and a cup of coffee for himself. She took time for breakfast. Outside snowflakes were coming down.

"I take the milk into town now. Those horses you saw in the corral yesterday were slated for the Friday run. I wasn't going to go, but I could."

"What are you saying, Ben?"

"That you should take Max. You'll be catching the same boat, the *Pontiac*. Josh should be in town already. I thought about it all night, Sarah. I'll leave Ma a note and meet you at the levee. I can see Max aboard and care for him, even bring him along to Baltimore if you could get him to Washington from there. That is, if you want him."

"Oh, Ben!" Sarah hugged her brother. "I could ride him there if I have to! And I could always stable him in Washington. You would do that for me?"

"Wouldn't want Kunkle to have Max," he said, "anymore than I'd want him to have Mose. Wouldn't want

Kunkle to sell Max to the army, either. I'll take your rental horse along to town and return him. You'd best get going now. I've got Max saddled. I've got to get to the milking."

Sarah was on her way in ten minutes. The weak November sun was just a red streak over the mountains in the east when she rode away from the farm on Max. Her head was clear because she knew what she was doing was right. But her heart was muddled, torn.

Behind her she left her past. It spilled out of the light from her mother's bedroom, where her mother was now dressing for the day. Her mother, who always said there was a price for everything. Would things be different if her mother had been willing to pay that price?

They would be different for Sarah. Was the price worth it?

She was already paying it. She knew, in the realization that she might never see her mother again. She wondered what Ma would say when Ben told her that the man sitting across the table from her last evening had been her missing daughter.

She was already paying it hearing Mose's bark in the falling snow. Begging her not to leave. Begging her to stay. Cutting into her.

Sarah pressed her knees into Max's sides, drew her beaver collar up around her, and went at a half-trot toward town.

Author's Note

During the American Civil War, many women ran off to fight as men for both the Union and the Confederate armies. Their reasons were as varied as their backgrounds. The tradition of American women fighting in wars goes back to the American Revolution, when such well-known women as Deborah Sampson, Margaret Corbin, and Nancy Hart fought for their country.

But many who fought in the Civil War expressed admiration for one woman who goes back a lot further than that — Joan of Arc, who led an army in France into combat in the fifteenth century. Loreta Janeta Valazquez, who served as a Confederate officer in the Civil War said, "My imagination fires with a desire to emulate the glorious deeds of Joan of Arc, the Maid of Orleans."

According to scholarly research, over a hundred women fought as men in the Civil War. And what about the ones we don't know of, the ones who kept their identity secret to their death, either on the battlefield or in their later years? Nobody knows how many of them served their country.

Why did women do this? Those who in later years spoke of their adventures cited patriotism and the desire to step out of the restricted role alloted to women at the time and do something daring.

Signing on as a recruit in the mid-nineteenth century was a lot easier than it would be today. Physical exams were cursory; indeed some recruits got in without seeing a doctor at all. The armies of both North and South needed men, especially after the first two years of the war, and recruiting sergeants were known to look the other way if someone was under eighteen. In looking the other way, perhaps they did not realize that the recruit was a woman.

Added to this was the fact that life back then was hard for some women from far-flung regions. They worked on farms, and household labor was backbreaking and relentless, so they built up their strength and were accustomed to difficult tasks, as were they used to riding horses and shooting guns. The routine of camp life presented no problems.

One must also understand that people, in general, were deeply committed to their "cause" back then, whether it was the cause of the Confederacy or that of the Union. Because medicine was so primitive and death constantly waited in the wings, religion was a part of everyday life and people were not distanced from their moral center. Also, religion and patriotism were closely entwined. They answered, every day, to their God and their spiritual selves. Patriotism was part of it all, and was nothing to be hidden away or ashamed of. So women answered the call, knowing they were needed, not only as soldiers, but as nurses.

While Sarah Wheelock is a character of my own invention, I have based her somewhat on "Franklin Thompson," the male alias for Sarah Emma Edmonds, one of the most famous male soldier impersonators in the Civil War. I did this partly because Sarah Edmonds served with the 2nd Michigan Infantry Regiment, and I could follow, historically, the action this regiment took in the war, from its arrival in the federal capital in mid-June 1861, where it was encamped on Washington Heights.

Also the 2nd Michigan appealed to me because it was "home" for at least three women who served. Anna

Etheridge was a "daughter of the regiment," a term given to women who went along as a woman, usually wearing a fancy uniform, leading the soldiers in parades, and in combat serving as a nurse and healer.

Jane Hinsdale was also in this regiment. She went to war alongside her husband, served as a nurse and was taken prisoner at 1st Bull Run. And Sarah Emma Edmonds was a woman who went as a soldier.

In a book she later penned about her army experiences, the real Sarah Emma Edmonds described herself as "soldier, nurse, and spy." She did go through Confederate lines to gather information, once disguised as a black man digging fortifications, another time as an Irish peddler. She did go on missions to obtain much-needed medical supplies, but her tenure in the army was longer than my Sarah's, and she never served with the Pinkerton detective agency. She came from Canada and when she paid a visit home, still disguised as a man, she relented and gave away her identity to her mother.

That is as far as the similarity between Sarah Wheelock and Sarah Edmonds goes. I have invented all the rest of the characters, with the exception of Abraham Lincoln, General McClellan, Doctor Hammond, Allan Pinkerton and his operatives, and Rose Greenhow and the women spies incarcerated with her at Fort Greenhow. Pinkerton's detective agency was active at this time in Washington City, and when I first conceived of the idea of my Sarah's working for him, I was not even sure he employed women. Imagine my delight when, on a trip to the library to look up his history, I discovered that he did! Allan Pinkerton used women detectives as far back as in 1856, half a century before they were recruited by the New York City Police Department.

Rose Greenhow, the famous Southern spy, was arrested in Washington City at this time, after being under surveillance by Mr. Pinkerton and his men and women. The Pinkerton detectives I use all actually existed at the time and served in the positions in which I've placed them, including the operative Timothy Webster, who was hanged by the Confederates.

Allan Pinkerton was an abolitionist who at one time ran an Underground Railroad way station in his home in Illinois, and in the 1850s broke the law by helping John Brown and other abolitionists to get runaway slaves into Canada.

His was the first detective agency in the United States. In the period after the war his agency became national as the country expanded. The postwar era was notorious for lawlessness. The country was growing too fast, the railroads were making inroads, and many Confederate ex-soldiers, whose one skill was fighting and killing, organized themselves into guerilla gangs, robbing banks and railroads and terrorizing many small towns in the midwest and west.

Pinkerton and his operatives engaged such outlaws as the Youngers, Jesse James, and the Reno brothers, as well as the Molly Maguires, an Irish terrorist organization intent on plaguing the miners in Pennsylvania.

Allan Pinkerton's sons, William and Robert, took over the agency in 1877. Pinkerton himself died in July, 1884, and today the agency has more than two hundred fifty offices in twenty countries.

As for Rose Greenhow, the spy network she ran out of Fort Greenhow in Washington was so complicated that I could not do it justice in this book. It may seem to the reader of today's world that Pinkerton's methods of intelligence were primitive. One may ask, "If she was so dangerous, why were people allowed to enter and leave her house with such freedom?"

According to today's standards, the surveillance and security of the time were primitive, but Rose Greenhow held to the one foothold she had — that of being a woman. Just as women were not yet permitted to break out of the mold men had created for them, so they were encased protectively in it, honored, esteemed, and revered. Rose knew this and used her sex as protection for her subversive activities.

All the other women "spies" who came and went in Fort Greenhow actually existed. I have tried to be faithful to Rose Greenhow's character, after considerable research. And if it seems that Little Rose is too mature, I have only depicted her as history has her recorded.

What happened to Rose Greenhow and her little daughter? She was moved to Old Capitol Prison, where she and Little Rose lived until her trial in the spring of 1862. After her trial she was deported to Richmond, Virginia where she was greeted by cheering crowds. Confederate President Jefferson Davis sent her to Europe as a courier. She put Little Rose in convent school and stayed in Europe, collecting intelligence and writing her memoirs, until she was recalled in 1864. Returning to America on a blockade-runner, her ship, the *Condor*, was chased by a Union vessel but managed to reach the mouth of Cape Fear River outside Wilmington, North Carolina. After the *Condor* was grounded on a sandbar, Greenhow feared she would be captured. She convinced the captain to send her and two companions ashore in a small boat.

The lifeboat overturned in stormy seas and Rose Greenhow drowned. She is buried in Wilmington, North Carolina.

For purists who will question many of the incidental items in this novel, let me explain that Sarah Wheelock's hometown of Casey's Mill, Michigan, is fictional. However, there was a Fort Wayne in Detroit where the army trained, though readers will immediately identify Fort Wayne with the state of Indiana.

For clarification, Bull Run and Manassas were the same battle. Most of the battles of the Civil War were given different names by the North and the South. The North named the battles after the nearest body of water, the South after the nearest town.

One of the dangers of writing a historical novel is the possibility that readers will put their twenty-first century perspective on the book. The inherent danger in writing a novel on the American Civil War is that, in the interest of being historically correct, the writer takes the risk of being politically incorrect and offending twenty-first century sensibilities.

For this reason I cite the speech patterns of the escaped slaves in Chapter Ten as being culled from historical research, from the accounts Sarah Emma Edmonds recorded in her book, *Soldier, Nurse and Spy.*

Also, historical research cites Rose Greenhow calling Allan Pinkerton "that German-Jew detective." He was neither German nor a Jew and she knew it, but was obviously letting her anger show in her prejudice.

Bibliography

Catton, Bruce. "A Michigan Boyhood." *American Heritage* 23, February 1972: pgs. 4–7, 81–84; April 1972: pgs. 33–41, 105; June 1972: pgs. 36–41, 92–96; August 1972.

Dannett, Sylvia G.L. *Noble Women of the North.* New York, NY: Thomas Yoseloff, 1959.

Denney, Robert E. *Civil War Medicine: Care and Comfort of the Wounded.* New York, NY: Sterling Publishing Co., Inc., 1994.

Edmonds, Sarah Emma. *Soldier, Nurse and Spy: A Woman's Adventures in the Union Army.* DeKalb, IL: Northern Illinois University Press, 1999.

Green, Constance McLaughlin. *Washington: A History of the Capital, 1800–1950.* Princeton, NJ: Princeton University Press, 1962.

Hall, Richard. *Patriots in Disguise: Women Warriors of the Civil War.* New York, NY: Marlowe & Co., 1994.

Hennessy, John. *The First Battle of Manassas: An End to Innocence, July 18–21, 1861.* Lynchburg, VA: H.E. Howard, Inc., 1989.

Leonard, Elizabeth D. *All the Daring of the Soldier: Women of the Civil War Armies.* New York, London: W.W. Norton & Co., 1999.

Leech, Margaret. *Reveille in Washington 1860–1865.* New York, NY: Grosset's Universal Library, 1941.

Long, E.B., with Barbara Long. *The Civil War, Day by Day: An Almanac, 1861–1865.* Garden City, NY: Da Capo Press, 1971.

Mackay, James. *Allan Pinkerton, The First Private Eye.* New York, NY: John Wiley & Sons, Inc., 1996.

Rhodes, Elisha Hunt. *All for the Union: The Civil War Diary and Letters of Elisha Hunt Rhodes.* New York, NY: Vintage Books, 1985.

Ross, Ishbel. *Rebel Rose: Life of Rose O'Neal Greenhow, Confederate Spy.* New York, NY: Harper & Brothers, 1954.

Safire, William. *Freedom.* New York, NY: Doubleday & Co., 1987.

A Sense of History: The Best Writing from the Pages of American Heritage. New York, NY: Houghton Mifflin Co., 1985.

Werner, Emmy E. *Reluctant Witnesses: Children's Voices from the Civil War.* Boulder, CO: Westview Press, 1998.

About the Author

Ann Rinaldi is an award-winning author of historical fiction for young people. Her novel, *Wolf by the Ears*, was named an American Library Association Best of the Best Books for Young Adults published in the last twenty-five years. *In My Father's House* was an ALA Best Book and Children's Book Council/International Reading Association Young Adult Choice.

Ms. Rinaldi is also the author of *The Quilt Trilogy*, a saga about three generations of an American family; *The Second Bend in the River*, an American Bookseller Pick of the Lists; and most recently, *Mine Eyes Have Seen* and *Amelia's War*. Ann Rinaldi lives in Somerville, New Jersey, with her husband.